Candleglow
and
Mistletoe

Josie Riviera

All Rights Reserved

Candleglow and Mistletoe

Copyright © 2016

Josie Riviera

PRAISE AND AWARDS

USA TODAY Bestselling Author

READER REVIEWS:
CANDLEGLOW AND MISTLETOE

*"I loved this story from the very beginning!
Noelle was so focused. It was great to watch Gabe
pull her out of her shell. I could feel her vulnerability
and also her determination to be the strong person she
truly was. Gabe...sigh! Gabe was pretty much the
perfect hero! This is the first thing I've read by Josie
Riviera. I am very excited to read more of her work!"*

*"This is an interesting Christmas romance short
story. I loved every minute of it! Loved the attraction
between Gabe and Noelle and how they need a second
chance for love."*

*"This was such a wonderful read, and I know I'm
going to read it again during the Christmas season.
Being a pianist, I could relate to the stress of stage
fright and how every day events can affect one's*

focus, but this is just one small element of the story. I love how the author weaves the 2 main characters together, and you quickly love and root for them to be a couple. There were some twists and turns, but they got there! Loved it."

READER REVIEWS: SEEKING PATIENCE

"Seeking Patience was an incredible book - it's a must read! I recommend it to any romance lover - they will love it!"

"Once you start reading you won't be able to put this novel down."

READER REVIEWS: SEEKING CATHERINE

"I find stories which explore cultural differences interesting and this writer does an excellent job. Opposites attract in this novel for an interesting plot."

"I loved this. What a terrific escape. I got into it and had a hard time stopping! I needed that, thanks!"

READER REVIEWS:
A SNOWY WHITE CHRISTMAS

"A SNOWY WHITE CHRISTMAS is sure to put you in the Christmas spirit. You can't help but fall in love with all the characters and get caught up in their lives. I can easily see this wonderful novella becoming a Hallmark Movie. Once I started reading I could not put this heartwarming story down. Josie Riviera gives you such a well-written story of Margaret and Fernando that you can't help but feel as if they are old friends of yours as you are reading. I cannot wait to read more by this wonderful author."

"What a lovely story about Christmas in the north. Very well written and full of emotion. I particularly enjoyed the characters, Margaret, Fernando, little Amelie and her menagerie of handicapped pets. I started reading and couldn't put the book down until I finished it. A wonderful read for Christmas."

READER REVIEWS: I LOVE YOU MORE

"Josie Riviera sure knows how to write heart tugging emotional stories and my only complaint is that I wish this awesome tale was longer. I was

instantly invested in all the characters' lives and was cheering for all of them and the struggles they were dealing with. I can't wait to read more by Ms. Riviera."

HALLMARK MOVIE QUALITY! "Fortunately I had an evening free because when I started reading I Love You More I did not want to stop. Josie pulls you right into the lives of Anastasia, Soo-Min and Luciano. In just a few sentences you feel as if you know them and can understand their feelings and reactions. I fell in love with these characters and when I finished I wished there was a sequel to read. I like that it was a short (2-2 1/2 hour) read but felt like a full novel in story line. I look forward to reading more of Josie Riviera's work."

TABLE OF CONTENTS

To my patient husband, Dave, and our three wonderful children.

CHAPTER 1

Noelle Wentworth never liked long bus journeys, especially when the bus was being driven by a preoccupied driver who kept glancing down at his cell phone. She shifted in the worn bus seat and fished through her purse for dry soda crackers to calm her motion sickness. Then she pushed down the impulse to march to the front of the bus and suggest that the bus driver slow his speed and concentrate on the snowy, frozen road ahead.

She glanced out the window. The traffic lights in Fisher's Crossing, the last small town before Snowing Rock, North Carolina, would force the driver to slow.

Noelle leaned back in her seat and blew out an exhausted breath. She'd been traveling since morning and longed to unpack, enjoy a long, hot shower, then practice piano for her upcoming concert.

She glanced at Anjali, the sleeping, five-year-old girl she'd met a few hours earlier. She'd started talking to Noelle, and Noelle had invited the little girl to sit in the empty bus seat beside her. Noelle smiled at Anjali's mother, Mrs. Fernandez, seated across the aisle.

The woman nodded back, her gaze tired, her hair graying at the temples. She zipped her long, red puffer jacket up to her chin and closed her eyes.

Noelle tucked her curly blonde hair beneath her hat, envisioning the picturesque town of Snowing Rock ahead. The town had been listed as one of America's top ten 'Christmas Towns' because of its quaint charm. She hoped nothing had changed in the fifteen years since she'd last visited. Although this wasn't a visit, she corrected herself. She'd agreed to temporarily manage her Aunt Joy's candle shop while her aunt convalesced from a hip injury.

Noelle's orderly private life would be disrupted for a few weeks while she helped out her aunt, but Noelle had agreed, purely out of duty. Although she was busy preparing for her concert, there was no other family, and her aunt needed someone she could trust.

Noelle knew that feeling all too well. She'd lost her parents a year ago and missed their support and guidance, especially after her bad marriage, made even worse by her illness. Along the way, Noelle had learned a hard lesson. She was leery of trusting anyone.

Absently, Noelle ran her fingers across her lap in silent piano arpeggios. Her upcoming concert was only a few weeks away. She fidgeted, pushing away the worst-case scenarios rushing through her mind. Suppose she ran off the stage again? Suppose the audience hadn't forgotten what had happened last time? She'd be performing in the magnificent Forum Theater in Saint Augustine, calling attention to herself, leaving herself open to criticism.

She inhaled deeply, then exhaled. No worries. As the months had gone by and she'd agonized over each excruciating detail of her previous, embarrassing performance, she'd rationalized that the experience had made her stronger.

3

She'd oversee Aunt Joy's candle shop during the day, and practice on her aunt's piano in the evening. Besides, a quiet, restful break from hectic Saint Augustine was exactly what Noelle needed.

When she returned to the stage, she'd be well rested and well-practiced, proving to Colin Rudovich, her ex, that she was once again a professional concert pianist who captivated her audiences. This time in Saint Augustine, there'd be no memory lapses. This time, a disturbing doctor's report wouldn't interfere with her concentration. Fortunately, the cyst on her ovary had been removed and the biopsy had found the cyst wasn't cancerous.

Coils of smoke drifted from the chimneys of gable-roofed bungalows as the bus idled at a stoplight in Fisher's Crossing. The light changed from red to green, and the bus picked up speed, whizzing by snow-covered, jagged rocks.

The whine of cold winter air seeped through the bus's window. Noelle gratefully breathed in the fresh air and closed her eyes, hearing the beginning bars of her Chopin concert piece.

"Miss Noelle, want me to sing 'Rockin' Around the Christmas Tree'?" Anjali tugged on

Noelle's sleeve. "My Daddy taught me all the words."

Noelle opened her eyes to Anjali's almond gaze.

"Sure, that's a fun Christmas song." Noelle glanced at her watch, then back at Anjali. "Aren't you tired? You've only slept a half hour since we got on eight hours ago."

Anjali's dark-complexioned face fell into a frown. "My Mommy said I don't need much sleep."

Noelle smirked. "I agree with her."

From across the aisle, Mrs. Fernandez laughed aloud. "My husband dotes on her. She sings all the time and he's encouraged her to join Snowing Rock's kindergarten choir next year."

Noelle felt that familiar, lonely ache in her gut. She swallowed her desolation and summoned a cheerful smile. "I remember hearing the choir when I attended Snowing Rock High. And I loved the sound of the children's voices blended together."

"Do you know how the song starts, Miss Noelle? You can sing with me." Anjali snapped her small fingers and began singing, "Rockin' Around the Christmas Tree ..."

Sleet tinkled against the window pane and Noelle glanced outside just as the bus flew by the last street sign in Fisher's Crossing.

She stood. "I'll be back, Anjali. The driver should reduce his speed. He may not know these mountain roads, but I remember them."

"Miss Noelle," the little girl asked, "What comes after 'At the Christmas party hop?'"

"'Mistletoe hung where you can see,'" Noelle sang softly.

The girl pushed up her small glasses. "'Every couple tries to—'"

"The truck on the other side is swerving into our lane!" a man in the front of the bus shouted. "It'll plow right into us!"

A pair of oncoming headlights reflected the road's icy glare. A sharp blast of the rig's horn followed. The bus driver threw down his cell phone and jerked the steering wheel hard to the right. The brakes shrieked, the wheels skidded.

Anjali pressed her fists to her ears and wailed.

"Anjali!" Mrs. Fernandez shouted from across the aisle.

Noelle's head jerked toward the window. She instinctively held up her arm to prevent Anjali from pitching forward.

The bus swerved, veered off the road, and screeched to a stop.

Darkness. Smells of gasoline. Muffled crying.

No, this couldn't be happening. With her heart racing, Noelle surveyed the darkened bus. Thankfully, none of the passengers appeared hurt. The bus was upright, although passengers crowded the aisle, tightening near the doors, pushing and shoving as they exited.

Noelle shot a glance across the aisle. Mrs. Fernandez's seat was empty.

"We need an ambulance!" the bus driver shouted into his cell phone.

Tears coursed down Anjali's dark cheeks. "Miss Noelle, where's Mommy?"

"We'll find her." Noelle slung her purse over her shoulder and squeezed Anjali's small hand reassuringly. They both jumped at the sounds of crunching metal as the bus sank deeper into the snow near the edge of an embankment. Several passengers screamed.

Stay calm, Noelle told herself. Stay calm. She brushed at a wetness on her forehead and noted blood on her fingertips. Now where had that come from? Perhaps she'd hit her head when the bus had swerved.

7

Through the clamor, she and Anjali pressed through the crowd and exited the bus. Fortunately, Noelle had picked up some winter clothing online before her trip. Their boots crackled on the icy snow as they made their way to the other passengers standing at the edge of an embankment. Several pointed to a gully, their conversations quiet and anxious.

Noelle peered past the edge and her chest tightened. The broken body of Anjali's mother in her familiar, red, long, puffer jacket, lay sprawled at an odd angle.

Noelle held in a gasp. Mentally, she chastised herself. Why hadn't she warned the bus driver sooner, insisting he slow his speed?

"Miss, do you need any help?" A deep male voice sounded through the crowd.

Noelle swung around.

A tall man, easily over six feet and sporting the beginnings of a dark beard, approached her. "Are you two all right?" he asked.

"Yes, yes I think so," Noelle said.

He was lean and extremely fit, wearing an olive-green parka and gray wool hat. "I'm parked there." He pointed to a black Land Rover on the side of the road. "I was driving behind the bus and my heart hit my throat when the driver took that last curve so fast." He stepped forward and touched his gloved hand to Noelle's forehead. "You're bleeding."

Self-conscious, she stepped back and tugged her hat lower over her forehead. "I must've hit my head on the window next to my seat."

The man's dark brows drew together. He drew a white cotton handkerchief from his parka and gently wiped her forehead. "Hold this on the cut to stop the bleeding," he said.

"Thanks. I'm okay, really." Taking judicious note of Anjali's quivering jaw and tear-stained face, Noelle dabbed at her forehead with his handkerchief, then handed it back to him.

"This is Anjali, and she's more important than my cut forehead." Noelle dropped her voice to a whisper and signaled toward the gully. "Anjali's mother ..."

"My Mommy fell down that big hill and she's hurt really bad!" Anjali's thin face pinched with tears. Her teeth were chattering and she shoved her tiny hands into her coat pockets.

The man knelt beside her. "I'll bring your Mommy back safely." He secured Anjali's pink beanie securely over her ears and offered a comforting smile.

"Promise?" Anjali sniffed.

"Yes. I'm a man of my word. You stay here with this woman, all right?" He came to his feet and nodded to Noelle.

Before Noelle could reply, he'd climbed over a guardrail and inched down the steep, icy embankment. He pulled his cell phone from his parka, lighting a path with his phone's flashlight.

Noelle stamped her frozen feet. Winter weather had smothered the mountain and had left a chilling, dark calmness. Trees groaned under the weight of the snow. She smoothed Anjali's wet hair from her cheeks and zipped the purple parka up to Anjali's chin.

A growing crowd gathered, cheering the man on. He'd reached Mrs. Fernandez, grabbed a branch, and fixed a splint beneath her leg.

An ambulance flashed to the scene and braked to a halt. Two paramedics leapt from the vehicle, shouted inquiries, then raced down the embankment carrying a stretcher. With the help from the bearded man, they shifted Mrs. Fernandez onto the stretcher and hoisted her up the embankment.

Noelle stopped one of the paramedics as he hurried past. "This little girl is Anjali and she's the injured woman's daughter."

10

"The woman's leg might be broken, her pulse is weak, and she's shivering. We're transporting her by ambulance to Snowing Rock Hospital," the paramedic replied without stopping.

"No! No!" Anjali screamed. "Ambulances scare me!"

"Ambulances scare me, too," Noelle admitted. "However, we need to get you to the hospital to be with your Mom."

"Sorry, we don't take kids," the paramedic said over his shoulder. "And only one person can ride in the cab."

The engine of the ambulance started, the flashing red lights triggered.

"Mommy, don't leave me!" Anjali broke free from Noelle and darted toward the ambulance.

The man in the olive-green parka caught Anjali as she dashed by. He bent to her height and gently grasped her forearms. "Mommy isn't leaving you. The doctors will make her better." He spoke with quiet, relaxed confidence. "I'll carry you to my SUV, and we'll follow the ambulance. Your friend will stay with you once we get to the hospital. All right?" He glanced at Noelle.

Noelle swallowed, her mouth dry. "I ... I haven't stepped into a hospital since—"

The man raised a dark brow, then bent to Anjali. "Do any of your aunts and uncles live in Snowing Rock?"

"My Aunt Nancy and Uncle Joe Fernandez live next door to us," Anjali said.

"Good. We'll call your aunt and uncle when we reach the hospital."

"No! I don't wanna go to the hospital. I'll wait for Aunt Nancy and Uncle Joe to come get me here."

The man looked toward the road, shining like polished ice beneath a round November moon. "The hospital is a better place to meet your aunt and uncle. Then everyone will be safe."

Anjali crossed her arms. "No!"

He wiped the snow icicles dripping from her nose with his handkerchief and took hold of her hands. "Why aren't you wearing gloves on such a wintry night?"

She pulled from his grasp and scratched her red, raw hands. "My Mommy forgot to pack them and she was really sad about it."

"I'm sad, too, because your hands are so cold. Take my gloves. That'll make Mommy happy and you can show her the gloves at the hospital." He removed his thick leather gloves, guided her small fingers into them, and grinned. "Do you want my parka next?"

"No! Your parka's too big for me. So are your gloves!" Anjali giggled and flapped her fingers. "I'll go to the hospital if you carry me and Miss Noelle can come, too."

"Miss Noelle?" He stiffened for a moment, flicked a glance in Noelle's direction, and smiled. He had strong, handsome features and hazel eyes.

Something about the admiration in his smile, the hint of gold specks in his hazel eyes, stirred her memory.

He cleared his throat and brought Anjali to his broad chest. "It's all right to be scared."

With Anjali in his arms, he called to one of the paramedics climbing into the back of the ambulance. "We'll follow you, Stan."

"These roads are hazardous. Maintain a safe speed, Mr. Waters," the paramedic said.

"I drive slow when I'm not working." The man regarded the snow-studded tires on his Land Rover. "I've traveled these roads many times and I'm prepared for every emergency."

As they made their way to his vehicle, Noelle said, "Thanks for reacting so quickly and so bravely."

He shrugged. "I do this for a living."

"You drive fast or you save people?"

He paused, studying her with open interest. "I act brave."

She blinked and studied him in return. His features were tanned and he probably spent a great deal of time outdoors, whereas she hardly ventured farther than her front porch. Still, something about him tugged at a long-ago memory.

She rubbed her lips and shook her head. Impossible, considering their apparently different lifestyles.

He held out his hand. "I'm Gabe. Gabe Waters, by the way."

"I'm Noelle Wentworth."

He clasped her hand and smiled warmly.

She glanced around. "Do we know each other? Your name sounds familiar."

He dropped his hand and rubbed his bristled chin. "Are you staying in Snowing Rock?"

He hadn't answered her question.

"I'm managing my Aunt Joy's candle shop for a few weeks," Noelle said. "I'll be living in her cottage while she convalesces from a hip injury in the town's rehab center."

"I love Snowing Rock. The town's beautiful, especially at Christmas."

"Have you lived in Snowing Rock a while?" she asked.

"I was in California for a few years, although I moved back to Snowing Rock because I always felt the town was my true home."

"The cool temperatures will be a welcome change from Saint Augustine," Noelle remarked. And she'd have plenty of time to perfect her performance pieces.

Gabe's gaze swung sharply. Lights flashing, the ambulance was speeding up the icy mountain road towards Snowing Rock. "We need to follow them," he said.

A battering gust of wind hastened their steps as they hurried to his Land Rover. Promptly, he buckled Anjali into the child seat in the back.

"You have children?" Noelle asked.

Inwardly, she chided herself for asking a stranger such a personal question. Judging by

15

his rugged appearance, he was probably a mountain man, married with a dozen kids.

"No children," he replied. "My cousin, Holly, flies here often from Virginia and she's the proud single parent of a four-year-old son, Devin."

Gabe grabbed an army surplus wool blanket from the trunk and wrapped the blanket around Anjali's legs. Despite the icy conditions, he strode with ease to the passenger side and opened the door for Noelle.

"Sorry, I only have one blanket," he said.

Noelle sank into the luxurious leather seat of his Land Rover and fastened her seat belt. "I thought you were prepared for every emergency?"

His eyes twinkled with a hint of mischief as he closed her passenger door. "I'm only one person and assumed I only needed one blanket."

He slipped into the driver seat and started the Land Rover, adjusting the heater to full blast.

"Better?" His smile was directed at Noelle, that comforting smile he'd used earlier with Anjali.

Noelle snuggled into the seat. "Perfect."

She glanced at his profile. His nose was straight, his jaw authoritative, yet his body language was gentle.

He eased his SUV onto the road, coasted through a hairpin curve, eased up on the gas when the vehicle slipped, then sped up slightly before reaching the steep incline.

A few minutes later, his Land Rover idled quietly at the entrance to Snowing Rock Hospital before he switched off the engine. He skirted from the vehicle and unfastened a sleeping Anjali from the child seat.

"Will you be all right from here?" he asked, coming around to the passenger side to open the door for Noelle.

She took his hand and stepped from the SUV. "It might be better if you brought Anjali—"

"I may be needed at the accident scene. Is your luggage on the bus?"

"Yes." Noelle nodded. "And my piano music's in a separate suitcase stowed beneath."

"I'll retrieve your luggage and tell the bus company to contact you." He lifted Anjali, preparing to place the child in Noelle's arms.

Noelle shifted and kept her arms at her sides. She shook her head. "Sorry, but—"

"But what? Didn't you say your aunt's recuperating in a rehab center?" he asked.

Noelle's body quivered from the cold. Her gaze darted to the daunting hospital, the brightly lit ambulance entrance sign. "A rehab center is different from a hospital."

He cuddled the sleeping child to his chest. "You acted very competently at the accident scene, Noelle. I'm sure you can sit in a hospital waiting room."

The hospital doors slid open as a wheelchair squeaked past. Smells of bleach along with stainless steel assaulted her nostrils, the same hospital odors she remembered from the night of her parents' deaths. Through the hospital window, Noelle saw two sweating and shivering women as they sat side by side and stared at her through the glass.

Noelle licked her lips and lowered her tone to a whisper. "I'm sorry. I can't go in."

Anjali snapped her eyes open. "Miss Noelle! I want to see Mommy!"

"I'll take you to see Mommy," Gabe said quickly. Noelle couldn't determine by his expression whether he was furious or disappointed with her.

She swallowed. She was putting her own selfish fears before the numerous accident victims who needed this man's help. Still, she couldn't control the panic welling inside her. She wasn't a nurse, she told herself. She wasn't capable of handling medical emergencies, or talking with doctors, or sniffing hospital antiseptic ...

She kissed Anjali's cheek. "I'll call the hospital to check on your Mommy as soon as I arrive at my aunt's cottage. I know you're in capable hands with Mr. Waters."

"Gabe," he reminded her.

"Yes, well, I'll be leaving, then, Gabe." Noelle rubbed the back of her neck. "My Aunt Joy lives at 10 Oak Street, and I remember her cottage wasn't far from the hospital."

"Oak Street is two blocks in that direction," Gabe pointed to a side street. "If you want to wait until Anjali's aunt and uncle arrive, I can drive you."

"No ... No, the walk will do me good after sitting on the bus all those hours." Noelle granted him a self-assured smile she didn't feel.

"Plug in my cell phone number in case you need anything while you're here."

19

"I'm sure I won't ... need anything. Thanks, anyway," she said.

"All right." He pivoted and strode through the hospital doors carrying Anjali in his arms.

A short walk afterward, Noelle reached her aunt's single-story cottage, where she gratefully thawed out her frozen limbs. She called her aunt to inform her that she'd safely arrived, brewed a hot cup of tea, and gratefully immersed herself in memorized piano pieces on her aunt's old, upright piano. She was determined to return to Saint Augustine and perform a triumphant concert.

Nothing, she decided as she played, could stand in the way of being well-prepared and conquering her paralyzing memory lapse once and for all.

Not even a freezing cold town, an out of tune piano, and a bus accident.

CHAPTER 2

In the space of a few seconds, all the memories of fifteen years ago had collided with the present when Gabe's gaze had connected with Noelle's shining, emerald eyes.

Noelle Wentworth. The cool, unattainable beauty who'd briefly attended Snowing Rock High. She was his high school crush and girl of his dreams, the brave young woman who'd lived in an affluent world he could only fantasize about. She'd been surrounded by classical music and nights at the opera. He'd been surrounded by poverty and sickness.

Nonetheless, in his senior year of high school, she'd impressed him with her courage.

He remembered the incident well, he thought with a grim smile. He was small, sickly with diabetes, and was constantly bullied. One of the biggest high school bullies had pushed Gabe into a locker, and Gabe had responded, ready to fight, arms upraised and fists clenched, although his heart had beaten madly in his chest.

Noelle had marched up and pried Gabe and the bully apart. With her jade-green eyes flashing, she'd scolded them both in a tone of frustrated impatience.

She hadn't known that her bravery had saved Gabe from a terrible beating, although he'd held his own in a fight with that same bully several months later. More importantly, Noelle had spurred Gabe to confront and manage his worst enemy, diabetes. Her intervention had provided the impetus for him to get strong.

An intercom paged a doctor, bringing Gabe's reflections back to the stuffy hospital waiting room. He shifted in line at the reception desk and jostled the dark-haired little girl in his arms.

Anjali snapped up her head and looked around. "Are my aunt and uncle here yet?"

"They'll come soon," he reassured, his memories drifting back to his remembrances of Noelle.

To his knowledge, Noelle hadn't flicked a glance in his direction after she'd broken up that fight. And why would she? He'd been the frail, skinny senior whereas she'd been the gorgeous, prim and proper freshman.

Gabe stepped to the hospital reception desk, aware of the clatter of computer keyboards combined with the smell of burned coffee.

"May I help you?" the receptionist asked.

"I'm checking on Mrs. Fernandez, who was brought here earlier in an ambulance," he said. "This little girl is her daughter, Anjali. We need to notify Anjali's aunt and uncle."

The receptionist poised her fingers over the keyboard. "Last name Fernandez?"

"Aunt Nancy and Uncle Joe," Anjali whispered loudly in Gabe's ear.

The receptionist searched the computer and tapped a phone number, speaking briefly on the phone. She laid the receiver on the cradle and said, "They're on their way. The hospital personnel will deal with insurance when they arrive."

"Thanks," Gabe said.

The receptionist offered a playful grin. "You're the stuntman from 'Force of Thunder

One'! I recognized you immediately, Mr. Waters. How long are you in town?"

"Indefinitely," he replied.

"Your newest movie, 'Force of Thunder Two', is being released on Thanksgiving Day. I have an extra ticket if you'd like to come with me."

"I never watch my films," he said.

Because he was simply the man on the screen, pretending to be someone else.

"I've heard you're a perfectionist." She handed him a pen and pointed to a sign-in sheet. "You're as handsome as any of those movie stars."

"Thanks." He grabbed the pen and her hand glanced over his. She smiled and twirled a strand of her hair.

He wrote his name on the sheet and handed her back the pen. "Let's get this little girl taken care of," he said.

In long, strides, he obligingly took a seat in the waiting room with Anjali in his arms.

ANJALI'S AUNT and uncle arrived at the hospital soon afterward, the proper insurance information was filled out, and Anjali was playing checkers with her cousins when Gabe departed.

Mrs. Fernandez had explained to Gabe and her family that when the bus had stopped so suddenly, she'd been jostled forward and had raced off in panic. She'd searched for Anjali in the darkness, unexpectedly slipped, and fallen down the snowy embankment.

After brief conversations with the nurses, Gabe learned that Mrs. Fernandez had been diagnosed with a displaced fracture. Her fracture would be splinted for at least a day to allow the swelling to subside, then casted.

"I'm impressed by what a brave girl you were tonight," Gabe complimented Anjali before he left. "I'll check on you and your Mommy in the morning. How about a high five to the side before I leave?"

Anjali giggled and slapped his hand hard.

With a quick wave to Anjali's aunt and uncle, Gabe returned to his vehicle.

He shifted his Land Rover to a lower gear and braked carefully as he made his way down the snowy mountain. He skidded a couple times on black ice and let up on the gas, carefully rotating his steering wheel back toward the road. Soon, he eased the Land Rover to a stop near two police cars.

He got out and strode to an officer photographing a roped off area. "Need any help?" he asked.

"The right shoulder metal beam stopped the bus from rolling down the embankment." The officer's wheezy breath puffed out warm steam in the cold air. "Some passengers suffered minor cuts and bruises, a few broken bones. The accident could've been much worse."

"I offered up a prayer for all the passengers. You know prayer helps," Gabe said.

"Do I?" The officer dismissed Gabe, then yielded toward the road. "Incoming traffic to Snowing Rock has been rerouted. You can either drive around the mountain and use the back roads to head back to town, or wait for the plow. They're scheduled to clear a path shortly."

"I'll wait." Gabe tramped through the snow to his Land Rover, feeling a slight dizziness. His heartbeat came rapid in his chest, a sure sign that he needed to eat and his blood sugar was dropping. He settled into his vehicle and opened the glove compartment. As he'd done hundreds of times since he'd been diagnosed with Type I diabetes, he pricked his finger and put a drop of blood on a test strip, then checked the results on a blood sugar meter that he kept in the inner pocket of his parka.

He peered at the near-blizzard conditions, the police ordering motorists to turn around because the unplowed, steep mountain road made traveling too dangerous.

Gabe rubbed his hands over his face and grabbed a granola bar from his pocket.

He couldn't afford to have his blood sugar drop too low again. Last time it had almost killed him.

CHAPTER 3

E ven from rehab, Noelle thought, Aunt Joy was a take-charge person, insisting her candle shop open promptly at nine o'clock every morning.

Conversely, Noelle had never been an early riser, especially the day after a traumatic bus accident that left her weak and slightly dazed. Her head hurt and a small bump had appeared on her forehead where Gabe had pressed his handkerchief to stop the bleeding.

Earlier that morning, Noelle had been pleased to find her two suitcases deposited at her aunt's front door. After downing two cups of coffee followed by a warm shower, Noelle had changed into a fisherman knit sweater and black skinny jeans. She carried her black leather flats in her tote bag and secured her curly blonde hair with two ivory hair combs.

She couldn't resist a quick scale warm-up, which promptly developed into a run-through of the entire Chopin two-piano arrangement.

Following a hasty C Minor finale chord, Noelle hurried out to walk three blocks to the candle shop. The gravel-gray skies were silent, the town bleached in a dazzling white snow.

Noelle reached the entrance to 'Scents of Joy' fifteen minutes later, pausing to admire the elegant fresh wreath topped by a long red velvet bow hanging on the shop's arched entrance door. She stepped inside and the aroma of beeswax, a subtle honey scent, greeted her nostrils.

"Hi!" A young woman waved from the opposite corner of the shop. "I'm Caroline Crockery." Caroline's short, red hair was highlighted by thin purple braids, her bangs cut awkwardly over her forehead. Clad in ripped blue jeans and a long-sleeved denim blouse, she topped her outfit with a white, ruffled apron and tied the long ribbons around her waist.

Caroline leaned forward on a wooden stool and regarded Noelle. "Yup, you have curly blonde hair and green eyes, so judging by your aunt's description, you're Noelle. Thanks for bringing our first official winter snowfall, Miss Saint Augustine."

Noelle responded with a smile, her gaze sliding meaningfully to the wall clock. "I apologize. I'm late for my first day of work."

"No worries. I'm glad you're here because this shop has been crazy busy."

"Do you know of a good piano tuner?" Noelle asked.

"That's an odd question. Oh right, you're a musician." Caroline put a hand to her mouth, her round face furrowed in thought. "Sorry. I don't play a musical instrument. Alan plays guitar, though. I can ask him."

"Who's Alan?" Noelle asked, walking to the back room to hang her coat and change from boots to flat shoes.

"He works at the pizzeria in town. He's a friend I met recently."

Noelle stepped back into the brightly lit shop. "I'll check for piano tuners on the internet tonight."

"The internet, as in the world-wide web?" Caroline amplified. "Good luck. Both the internet and lights go out a lot in this town because of the wintry weather."

Noelle shot a cautious glance at the customers beginning to file in. Here goes, she thought. She'd never had retail experience. She hurried to the cash register while Caroline measured a mason jar, then cut a length of wick two inches longer than the jar.

"My aunt told me you're the most dedicated part-time worker she's ever employed," Noelle said.

Caroline's brown eyes gleamed, reflecting her jolly smile. "A candle shop is my favorite place. It's so warm and cozy and the scents are wonderful, especially during the holiday season. Who doesn't love making candles?"

"Me, for one," Noelle raised her hand in reply while she surveyed the shelves overflowing with a vast array of candles in a variety of sizes and shades. "I've never made candles. Is it difficult?"

"Very easy," Caroline assured.

"When I visited this shop many years ago, it was much smaller and more sparsely stocked," Noelle said.

"Your aunt expanded her business last year using her retirement savings."

"She never mentioned anything to me." Noelle made a mental note to ask her aunt if she needed money. Noelle didn't have much to give because her concert engagements had been close to none for the past year, but any money she had she'd gladly share.

"Your aunt's a seventy-year-old entrepreneur," Caroline said. "She rented the adjoining shop's space so she could offer candle-making classes."

"Sounds like I have a lot to learn." Noelle retrieved a white, ruffled apron from behind the counter and tied the apron at the waist. "What should I do first?" she asked.

Caroline swept out her hand. "Hah! Where should I start?"

BY NOON, the shop was crowded with customers, and Noelle's hair had fallen from the ivory clips, hanging in unruly waves around her shoulders. She hadn't had a moment to tend to her hair, nor think, nor breathe. All the shop's details, including the appropriate music softly playing in the background, had been decided beforehand in meticulous notes left by Aunt Joy. The CD, featuring dulcimer and acoustic guitar playing an instrumental arrangement, had gone around for the fifth time.

Noelle apologized to a middle-aged woman standing at the cash register because Noelle had made her umpteenth mistake ringing up the customer's credit card. Inwardly, she rebuked herself. Perhaps her ex had been right. Perhaps she was inept at everything she touched. Perhaps the customers would begin judging her as harshly as the music critics had.

Caroline came to the register to correct Noelle's mistake, working briskly and efficiently. "That's Lucia Crandall," Caroline whispered, as an attractive woman, dressed in an elegantly tailored camel wool coat and brown suede leather boots, paraded into the shop. "Lucia owns Misty Mountain Candles, the other candle shop in town. Although her shop's doing extraordinarily well, she checks up on us once in a while—probably assessing her competition to remind herself she's still in the lead." Caroline shook her head. "We don't have her unlimited advertising dollars, although when I attend

NYU next year and earn my degree in market research, I plan to marry a rich banker and offer my expertise to your aunt." Caroline added, "Lucia's rich husband died last year."

"I'm sorry for her loss," Noelle said.

Caroline snorted. "You're probably sorrier than Lucia was."

"I'm surprised this small town can sustain two candle shops. When I lived here fifteen years ago—"

"Snowing Rock has become a trendy vacation hideaway for wealthy people from all over the world," Caroline interrupted. "Some have bought permanent residences here."

As Lucia waltzed to the cash register, Caroline beamed a bright, artificial smile. "Looking for anything special today, Lucia?"

"Nothing in particular." Lucia glanced at her stunning reflection in one of the shop's hanging mirrors and arranged her shining black hair to show off a stylish pixie cut. "You're Joy's niece?" Lucia asked Noelle.

"Yes, and it's good to meet you, Lucia," Noelle replied.

"Will you be kicking off your shoes and prancing around the shop barefoot like your slightly insane aunt?"

"I'll leave my shoes on, thanks, although I may only wear socks," Noelle recovered admirably.

"I assume you've had retail experience?" Lucia asked.

"None," Noelle said.

"Know anything about making candles?"

"Not a thing."

Lucia smirked. "This will be my most successful holiday season in years." She opened the lid of one of the candles on a nearby shelf, one of 'Scents of Joy's' handmade candy-cane candles. "The wick's too small for this candle's diameter, Caroline," Lucia pointed out. "You poured the wax too high. When the wax begins to change shape, stop pouring."

Caroline saluted Lucia. "Thanks for the tip."

"Did I mention I'm opening a second shop in New York City? My late husband's business originated there and I'm considering a store front on Fifth Avenue."

"Do keep us posted," Caroline replied. "We'll be waiting with bated breath."

Lucia made her way down the shop's aisles, examining price stickers on the bottom of each candle jar. "Joy and I enjoy a friendly rivalry," she said to one of the customers.

"Yeah, right," Caroline whispered to Noelle. "Friendly rivalry my —"

Noelle grinned. She glanced at her watch, counting the minutes until she could break for lunch. If she hurried to Aunt Joy's cottage and skipped lunch altogether, she could practice the difficult octaves in the Brahms sonata.

Just you wait, Colin, she thought, envisioning the smug face of her ex. I realize you're trying to exploit me again, although I'm ready this time because I've learned not to trust you. In fact, I don't trust anyone. She smiled just thinking about his heated features, his jaw dropping as they performed the crowd-pleasing opening measures of the Chopin duo-piano arrangement.

"When are the shop's candle-making classes?" one of the customers asked. Her question brought Noelle's musings back to the cash register.

Noelle lifted her shoulders and directed a quizzical brow toward Caroline.

"Every Saturday evening from now until Christmas," Caroline said. "Our candle-making class is free, although customers can purchase the supplies here on the first night of class. And we'll be serving hot chocolate and homemade sugar cookies."

Noelle twisted to Caroline. "Who's making homemade sugar cookies?"

"You are. I'll bring the hot chocolate. Your aunt said she was leaving her sugar cookie recipe in the cottage."

"I've never baked a cookie in my life."

"Just follow the recipe."

The woman who'd inquired about the candle-making classes inclined her head toward Noelle. "Your aunt must be so grateful that you were able to help her out. She's bragged about your accomplishments for years." The woman reached across the counter and patted Noelle's arm. "From what she's told us, you're a concert pianist. Can you play background music for our ladies' luncheon at Snowing Rock country club in December? That piano hasn't been played in years."

Noelle blinked. Once, she'd performed in large concert halls and commanded astronomical fees. That is, before her last dismal performance, because offers no longer flooded her email inbox. Perhaps, though, it had been partly her fault. She'd chosen to hide away in her apartment and had closed all her social media accounts after the performance, rendering herself virtually unreachable.

"I'm sorry I can't commit to any engagements," Noelle replied. "All my free time in Snowing Rock will be devoted to practicing. When I return to Saint Augustine, I'll share the concert stage at the Forum Theater with Colin Rudovich."

One of the customers at the register pressed her hands to her chest. "Mr. Rudovich is one of the finest pianists in the world! I've bought all his recordings!"

Noelle sighed heavily, said nothing, and finished counting the woman's change.

"I've heard praise regarding Noelle Wentworth's performances, also," a familiar, deep male voice rang through the shop.

Noelle snapped her head up. The shop grew quiet as Gabe Waters entered. He removed his sunglasses, placed them in his pocket, and pushed back his wavy chestnut hair. He'd shaved. She hadn't expected to see him again, but here he stood, looking tall, dark, and well ... extraordinarily handsome. He wore black fitted jeans and the same olive-green parka. His hazel eyes mesmerized her, and her feet decided to root themselves to the floor.

"Gabe?" Noelle asked. He was so masculine, with his broad shoulders and powerful build, and he seemed out of place in a candle shop wafting with feminine aromas of lavender and beeswax.

"I think so." He exaggerated a look around, then met her gaze. An unhurried smile worked its way across his features. "Did you get your luggage?"

"Yes, the bus company delivered my suitcases this morning." She paused, feeling her cheeks warm with embarrassment because of her panicked reaction at the hospital. "Sorry about last night ... I had so much on my mind."

She'd acted like a coward and had run off with no plausible explanation. For the past year, she'd fought hard to overcome her fears and insecurities, although she'd failed miserably at the hospital.

He held up a hand. "Perfectly understandable after the trauma of the bus accident. I could've driven you to your aunt's cottage if you'd been able to wait."

"You were needed in two places at once, the hospital and the accident scene," Noelle said. "You didn't need a third obligation when my aunt's cottage was within walking distance."

"You're not an obligation, Noelle."

"I called the hospital and a nurse told me that Mrs. Fernandez will be monitored a few more days," Noelle said. "How's Anjali?"

"She seemed fine when I left. She's staying with her aunt and uncle until her father gets back. He's been working out of town. Fortunately, kids are resilient."

"I plan on visiting both of —" Noelle began.

"I assume you'll wait until Mrs. Fernandez gets home to visit them," Gabe finished. They both smiled.

Lucia Crandall made a beeline for Gabe, wrapping her fingers around the slight, wispy side layers of her hair. "When did you arrive back in town, Gabe? You usually call me."

"I arrived a couple days ago," he replied.

Lucia playfully touched his sleeve. "Dinner at my place tonight?" she asked, her lilting voice loud enough for the entire shop to overhear.

He kept his gaze on Noelle. "I'll text you, Lucia."

"I'll be waiting," Lucia's hand lingered on his sleeve while she eyed Noelle with disdain. "I couldn't help overhearing, and the invitation to play for our ladies' luncheon at the country club next month still stands. I'm on the board and background piano music would be delightful."

Before Noelle could respond, Lucia strutted to the door, pausing at the shop's front window where Caroline arranged several cranberry glass votives on a silver tray, affixing pine cones and holly berries to the glass.

"One of your candles is smoking, Caroline. Your distributor used too much fragrance oil," Lucia said. She swiveled, gave a smart wave in Gabe's direction, and exited the shop.

Noelle sighed. "Everyone's a candle expert except me."

An enigmatic smile tugged at the corner of his lips. "And me."

She met his gaze. "May I help you find anything?"

His gaze warmed. "I'm shopping for my cousin, Holly. Remember I told you about her last night? Our dads were brothers. She's getting married on December twenty-second and I'm the only groomsman."

"And her little boy, Devin, is the reason you keep a car seat in your Land Rover."

"And Devin is the ring-bearer."

Aware of how quiet the shop had suddenly become, Noelle glanced around. Every customer seemed preoccupied with candles and pricing, although Noelle had the feeling they were

41

listening intently to every word of her conversation with Gabe.

"Holly wants to have both her wedding and reception at my place. I converted one of the old barns on my property into a large hall." Gabe grinned ruefully. "That is, if she doesn't change her mind, because she's canceled the wedding once already."

"Doesn't she want to get married?"

"She's the restless type. She's finishing a Master's Degree in Interior Design at Virginia Tech. She knows I'm a planner, and she's asked me to arrange the candle details."

"Candle details?" Noelle repeated.

He nodded. "She wants an evening candlelight ceremony and she's insisting on one particular scent from your shop." Gabe pulled a piece of paper from his wallet. "Candleglow and Mistletoe."

"Your cousin has excellent taste because Candleglow and Mistletoe is our signature holiday fragrance." Caroline held up a deep-green candle and waved Noelle and Gabe over to the display. "There's notes of sandalwood and vetiver in the aroma."

"I'm not sure what vetiver is, although I detect a hint of cedar and fir trees. The scent is woodsy and a little sweet." Noelle laughed and held up the jar. "At least that's what the description says." She handed the candle to Gabe.

He sniffed and shrugged. "My house is in the woods, and my cousin wanted a Christmassy wedding, so this candle fits the bill."

Noelle laughed and walked to the cash register. "You're certainly easy to please."

He grinned, the dimple on his chin prominent. "Whatever makes my cousin happy. I'm overprotective of her, but she's marrying a great guy. His name is John and they're crazy about each other. He's responsible and stable and he'll be a good father to Devin."

A few minutes later, Gabe took his place at the back of the cash register line, his arms laden with a dozen Candleglow and Mistletoe candle jars. When he stepped to the register, he placed the candles on the counter and handed Noelle his credit card. "I'm setting up six long tables for the reception and will put two or three candles on each, so I'll need a half dozen more. I'll pay for all of them now. Some of them I may put aside as extra gifts for Holly."

Caroline called from the display window. "Candleglow and Mistletoe is in short supply because we keep selling out, but we should be able to get more in. Let me check." She disappeared into the back room.

Noelle bit her lip and attempted to appear confident. "Would you like these candles gift-wrapped?" she asked crisply. She was all thumbs when it came to wrapping gifts.

"Yes, please."

Fortunately, the transaction went smoothly. Uttering silent appreciation to the heavens above, Noelle handed Gabe back his credit card and thanked him for his purchases.

She glanced at the clock. Twelve fifteen. At this rate, she'd never break for lunch and practice octaves. She whirled, measuring and cutting festive gold paper, wrapping each candle separately. She tied on bright satin-red bows, stepped back, and smiled approvingly. Not bad for a beginner, she decided.

"Very nice, Noelle. Thank you," Gabe said with a grin. "Now I'd like to take you to lunch."

Adamantly, she shook her head. "Thanks, but I'm too busy."

"There are details about my cousin's wedding I can't begin to comprehend and I'd appreciate a competent, beautiful woman's advice," he said.

44

Her smile faded. "You picked out the candles."

"Even I know there's more to a wedding than candles."

Yes, Noelle thought. There was commitment in good times and in bad.

And trust, feeling certain that she could rely on her husband, assured that he would be there for her. She sighed. All of that had been lacking in her marriage to Colin Rudovich.

Sadly, the word 'love' hadn't come to mind because, in hindsight, her relationship with her ex had been one-sided. She'd been impressed with his drive to succeed. He'd married her solely to further his career. After a time, she was just a pretty, crowd-pleasing accessory. The media had loved seeing the husband and wife duo perform together on the concert stage.

With a weak nod, Noelle said, "My dreadful marriage to a flamboyant, domineering concert pianist ended in divorce. You'll have to look elsewhere for wedding advice."

"Therein lies the problem," Gabe countered. "My dreadful marriage to a narcissistic, British film star ended in divorce. So. besides attending the same high school, we share something else in common. Our divorces."

CHAPTER 4

Before Noelle could ask what Gabe had meant by his high school comment, Caroline emerged from the back room.

"Bad news and good news, Mr. Waters," Caroline said. "The bad news is that Candleglow and Mistletoe candles are almost out of stock. The good news is I've been able to order more and the candles should arrive before Christmas."

"Thanks, Caroline." Gabe bestowed a charming smile. "If you don't anticipate the shop being busy for the next hour, I'd like to take your boss to lunch. I'll pick up the candles later."

Caroline waved toward the door. "Yup, not a problem. The shop quiets around this time and

I'll take my lunch when Noelle get back. If business slows this afternoon, I'll teach her how to make candles."

Noelle gulped back horrified laughter. "Do I really need to learn?"

Making candles seemed too difficult, involving wicks and hot wax and proper temperatures.

Caroline blithely flung Noelle's question aside. "Yes, if you want to teach our first class on Saturday night, Miss Saint Augustine."

A few beats later, Noelle pulled on her high boots and cream-colored jacket. Whirling a scarf around her neck, she tucked her hair beneath her knitted cap. "I can't be long for lunch because I want to practice Brahms," Noelle said, as Gabe guided her to the shop's doorway.

The charming smile lingering on his features vanished. "I won't take up much of your time. There's a sub place a few doors down and the service is quick." He pointed toward a building at the end of the street. "Do you want me to call ahead and place a rush order?"

He watched her closely, without a hint of animosity in his gaze.

She glanced uncertainly at him. "I'm sorry I was rude. There's no need to hurry."

The corners of his lips turned up, apparently mollified by her abrupt change of attitude. "You arrived in Snowing Rock last evening by a bus that crashed. Understandably, you're overwhelmed and preoccupied," he said.

A fierce blast of cold wind caused Noelle to lose her breath as she stepped onto the frozen sidewalk beside him. Her hair blew off her forehead.

Gabe gently touched her temple. "That bang made quite a bump."

She shrugged off his hand, pausing to regard her reflection in the candle shop's front window, adjusting her side-swept bangs to cover the bump. Then gliding past him, she slipped on the ice.

His hand shot out and captured her elbow. "Winter in Snowing Rock is a lot different from Saint Augustine. Fortunately, I'm here to save you from bus accidents and slick sidewalks." His white teeth flashed a leisurely, wide smile.

While they walked, Gabe kept a firm grip on her elbow. Noelle stopped to marvel at the streetlights decorated with holly and ivy. Bright purple bows glittered like sparkling icicles from each of the storefronts. She sniffed the fragrant, sweet smell of roasted chestnuts when they passed a street vendor. People stood in line, walking away with brown paper bags brimming with warm chestnuts.

"The town feels so Christmassy, although it's only early November," she noted.

"Snowing Rock is considered Christmas Town, remember?"

She tried to capture the memory nagging at her. "Have you and I met before?"

"If we did meet, I couldn't bear to imagine that I was so forgettable," he said softly.

She bit her bottom lip. "Before my parents and I moved to New York City, I attended Snowing Rock High for one year, when I was a freshman."

"And I was a senior and looked different fifteen years ago."

She nodded politely while pushing the notion that they'd ever met from her mind. She hadn't had time to date when she'd been in high school. All her free hours had been devoted to piano practice. That's why she needed to get back to Saint Augustine and perform, to prove to herself that all those practice hours hadn't been in vain.

Gabe brushed a snowflake from her face and reclaimed her elbow. He nodded toward the end of the street. "There's Hal's Subs. You can see the sign from here."

A few minutes later, he opened the door for her, guiding her inside the bustling restaurant, tipping his head to people as they passed. He stopped a teenage waiter and placed an extra order, giving an address Noelle didn't recognize. Then he accepted her coat, removed his parka, and hung their coats on a coat rack near their booth.

Noelle checked the time on her cell phone. If their order came quickly, she'd still have time to reach her aunt's cottage and practice Brahms.

"Coffee?" Gabe slid into the booth seat across from her and stretched his long legs beneath the table. He wore a v-neck navy blue sweater that emphasized his muscular build. He grabbed two menus and glasses of water from a passing waiter and handed a menu to her. "I recommend the whole-wheat turkey sub topped with grilled vegetables because it's the best in town."

Noelle perused the menu. "Thanks, but coffee and a chef salad is perfect." She regarded him, surprised he was sweating despite the cold weather. "You look pale," she remarked.

He shrugged. "I worked out this morning and probably pushed myself too far."

Preoccupied, she nodded and glanced at the time on her cell phone, calculating how long the waiter would take to revisit their table so they could place their orders. She curled her hands together beneath the table and darted Gabe a glance. He was smiling at her. She, on the other hand, was being bad-mannered to a man who'd been very kind. Didn't she at least owe him her attention during a short lunch?

The teenage waiter headed over, paper and pen in hand. After they'd finished ordering, Gabe leaned forward and asked, "How do you like working in your aunt's candle business?"

Noelle composed her features, unwilling to admit how under-qualified she felt.

"It's not the antiquated shop I remember from fifteen years ago," she said. "And Caroline mentioned that my aunt plans to continue the expanding, selling homemade beeswax candles online, and perhaps internationally."

Gabe grinned at her over the glass's rim. "Your aunt must be tech-savvy."

"She isn't, and neither am I." Noelle waved her hand dismissively at herself, then perched her chin on her hands. "What do you do for a living? I'm guessing you might be a lumberjack?"

51

"Why would you think that?"

She shrugged. "You seem so outdoorsy. I visualize you living in a cabin in the woods."

He smiled. "I'm a stuntman for feature films."

She blinked. He'd spoken so nonchalantly. The resultant beat of silence was punctuated by the hum of people's conversations and the juke box playing 'I'll Be Home For Christmas' sung by Bing Crosby.

Noelle laughed nervously. "You're a stuntman for famous actors who don't want to perform their own stunts?"

"Something like that."

"Isn't that a dangerous gig?"

He laughed softly. "The industry calls them gags, not gigs. Many stunt people are freelance and in order to keep their jobs, they don't publicize their injuries."

"Have you ever been injured?"

"I'm known for driving fast racecars."

He was hedging, she thought. "Racecars that crash?" she pressed.

Gabe focused on the teenage waiter preparing their food behind the counter instead of meeting her gaze. "I've leapt out of a burning car or two."

"Were you ever hurt?"

Gabe was unnaturally quiet for a moment.

She clasped her hands together in her lap and regarded him. "I'm sorry. I'm asking too many questions."

"I don't mind." He met her searching gaze. "And yes ... I was hurt once. The racecar I drove overturned and set fire. It was a treacherous, high-risk stunt and the accident occurred for two reasons. Partly because I lost control, and partly because a shortcut had been taken regarding safety precautions."

"Were you okay?"

He grinned. "I'm here, aren't I? And 'Force Of Thunder' was a box office hit."

"I've never seen the film," Noelle admitted. "Although I can't imagine ..."

He brushed his knuckles across her hand. "No one was seriously hurt. Afterward, the director was delighted because the shot was spectacular."

"The director should've been more concerned with safety issues than a box office hit."

"I agree."

Judging by his curt response, Noelle assumed the subject of safety and uncaring directors wasn't a topic Gabe was eager to pursue, so she grappled for a lighter subject.

"So, you work with famous movie stars?" she asked brightly.

"You name one of the multi-million-dollar action movies in the last five years, and I've probably been featured in a car chase or two."

The teenage waiter brought their sandwich, salad, and coffee. Noelle said grace and Gabe joined in. Then she placed her napkin on her lap and sipped her coffee.

"You should eat," Gabe said. "You had a long, distressing night and busy morning."

She picked up her fork and eyed the sumptuous array of lettuce, cold cuts, and sliced avocado before taking a bite.

Gabe concentrated on his sandwich. When he was finished, he said, "Tell me about the illustrious musical career you're known for when you're not running a candle shop."

She set down her fork. "As I mentioned, I'm performing in Saint Augustine on December fifteenth, so I'll only be in Snowing Rock a few weeks."

She tried to dispel the thoughts chattering through her mind—that no matter what she did or how hard she tried, the audiences would never forget her poor performance. After one memory lapse, she'd assumed her fans would rally around her. However, she'd learned she couldn't trust a fickle audience, making her fearful of counting on anyone.

Gabe's expression softened. "All that piano practice when you were a teenager paid off. I remember listening to you from the weight room at Snowing Rock High."

All she'd done in high school was practice chord balancing and scale technique. She'd never had a normal adolescence, never dated, never attended proms like the other girls.

Noelle's reflections were interrupted by the teenage waiter pouring her more coffee. She extended a 'thank you' and studied Gabe's rugged, chiseled face.

"I don't remember you, although you obviously remember me," she said.

"Your piano music from that practice room motivated me to bench press four hundred pounds. I decided if you could practice that hard, then I could work out in the gym even harder."

"What did you do when I played slow, dreamy, piano pieces like Debussy?" she joked.

His smiled widened. He reached across the table and claimed her hands in his. "I'd slow my pace to match yours and do five squat thrusts instead of ten."

Throughout the remainder of lunch, she sat straight and alert as Gabe shared his most dangerous stunts and exploits with her. He answered her questions promptly while she relished the food, enjoying the bustling, upbeat atmosphere of the sub shop. He was witty and charming. He made her laugh out loud, his light-hearted banter contagious.

When the waiter waded into their conversation and placed a check on the table, Noelle realized that she and Gabe were somehow still holding hands.

She pulled from his grasp. "I need to get back to my aunt's cottage and practice before I return to the shop." She stood and pulled her wallet from her purse.

Gabe stilled her hand. "Please. I insist on paying."

"No." She shook her head, immediately mistrusting his motives. She didn't want to owe him anything. "I'll pay for myself."

He looked genuinely annoyed. "I invited you, remember? And we never got to discuss my cousin's wedding. You can reciprocate next time."

"I'm sure all the details of the wedding have been planned perfectly." She handed him the money for her portion of the bill. "Sorry, but there'll be no next time. I'm returning to Saint Augustine in a month and between the candle shop and practicing, I'm too busy."

❄

AS HE ESCORTED Noelle to her aunt's cottage, Gabe shielded her from the wind by walking backwards in front of her. He shared hilarious tidbits about well-known movie stars, continuing to wave off the perilous aspects of his job.

When they reached the doorstep of her aunt's cottage, he told her that he'd be spending the remainder of the afternoon at an outreach center he'd recently opened for wayward teens.

"Would you like to see the center sometime?" he asked. "We're putting together a Christmas musical to give teens something to do and keep them off the streets. We could use your musical expertise."

"Perhaps."

"Good answer." He chuckled. "I'll call you at the shop, all right? In the meantime, take care of that bump." He waited for her to step into the foyer, then changed direction and strode down the street.

Inside her aunt's cottage, Noelle waited for the kettle to boil, folded her aunt's red crocheted blanket neatly on the flowered couch, then eyed the fireplace. How festive the wooden mantel would look decorated with fresh poinsettia plants, embellished with deep green Candleglow and Mistletoe candles flanking each corner.

Noelle leaned back on the couch, a surprising heaviness in her chest at the thought of leaving the cozy cottage, nestled in the pine trees, for her air-conditioned Saint Augustine high-rise.

What if she spent Christmas in Snowing Rock after her performance? She and Aunt Joy could hang two red burlap stockings on the mantel and decorate a pine-scented Christmas tree with multi-colored, twinkling lights.

Noelle hadn't celebrated Christmas since her parents had passed, because she hadn't had the heart for festivities. And Colin, her ex, hadn't been interested in Christmas, declaring the entire holiday commercialized and a waste of time.

She set her teacup on an end table, went to the piano, and adjusted the squeaky piano stool.

She tilted her head back and closed her eyes, visualizing the music before she played. Her hands struck a deep, resonant, bass octave, the last passage of the Brahms.

Her right foot pushed the damper pedal and something inside the piano snapped with a sharp cracking noise. The damper pedal stuck, the most important pedal on the piano, and every note of the bass chord she'd struck with gusto rang on and on.

She groaned aloud. The vertical rod must've fallen out.

On her phone, she searched the internet and found a listing for a piano tuner and technician in Fisher's Crossing. She called the tuner and left an urgent message.

Assuring herself she still had five minutes before reporting to the candle shop, she stretched out on her back and peered inside the piano.

She identified the problem and attempted to insert the pin back into the lever hole. The pin failed to cooperate, and she bumped her head as she slid out from beneath the piano.

Now what? Noelle closed her eyes for a moment, then stood and straightened.

Simple. As soon as she arrived at the cottage this evening, she'd try again. Because if the damper pedal couldn't be fixed, the piano was useless, and she couldn't practice.

She sank onto the couch and gulped an unsteady breath.

Her heartbeat raced at the thought of another failed performance on stage. If that happened, would her concert career truly be over?

CHAPTER 5

A fter Caroline checked out early the following day to see Alan at the pizzeria, Noelle planned to close the candle shop by six. Whenever she'd had a moment, she'd gone over in her mind the steps to fixing the piano's damper pedal. Perhaps she needed more light when she was beneath the piano. Perhaps she needed to consult an instruction manual. Perhaps she should try calling another piano technician.

She shook her head repeatedly. She'd only been in Snowing Rock a short while and she'd already lost valuable practice time.

Through endless false smiles, six o'clock sped to seven, and Noelle rang up the last customer of the evening. She congratulated herself on how adept she'd become at running the cash register in only one day. And the ledgers had tallied up perfectly.

In the darkness of a cold November night, Noelle walked the few blocks to the town's senior rehab center. Humming the opening Chopin melody softly to herself, she stopped at her aunt's room on the first floor, knocked once, and stepped inside.

"Noelle?" Aunt Joy sat in a wheelchair by the window and craned her head. She opened her arms and Noelle rushed into them. Her aunt's shoulders shook with weeping. "My dear niece, you look beautiful. You're so slim, so tall," Aunt Joy dabbed her eyes with a hot-pink fringed handkerchief she clutched tightly in her hands.

Noelle planted a kiss on her aunt's wrinkled cheek. Aunt Joy was the only family she had left, now that Noelle's parents had passed.

Noelle stepped back. "And you haven't changed a bit in fifteen years."

Aunt Joy wore a red, white, and blue tie-dyed tee shirt and no make-up except for bright blue eye shadow, which highlighted the pale blue of her eyes. Her long gray hair flowed over her shoulders and heavy green bohemian earrings dangled from her pierced ears.

Fresh tears stung Noelle's eyes. She'd missed her independent Aunt Joy, a woman who spoke her own mind. Surprisingly, she was beginning to feel very much at home here in this picturesque, quirky mountain town.

Coyly, her aunt slanted a straw fedora hat on her head. "Do you enjoy working at 'Scents of Joy'?"

"You'll be pleased to know that your shop was very busy." Noelle evaded the question. "As long as Caroline doesn't quit, everything will continue to operate smoothly."

"You're a capable young woman and I know I can rely on you as well, dear." Aunt Joy offered a convincing smile. "Although, I'll miss Caroline when she attends NYU next year. She's been offered a full scholarship."

Noelle met her aunt's engaging smile. "She plans to study marketing and marry a successful banker."

"Sounds like Caroline, planning her life in ambitious detail."

Noelle pulled off her cream-colored jacket. "Anyway, how are you feeling?" she asked.

"The doctor said I should be able to return to the shop by the first week of December. I've done enough physical therapy and rehab to last a lifetime and I'm ready to leave." Aunt Joy scraped a hand through her hair. "Do we need to order more inventory?"

"Probably by the weekend," Noelle replied. "Certainly Candleglow and Mistletoe candles are big sellers."

"I stocked more than a half dozen boxes of candles."

Noelle threw open the heavy draperies and gazed out at a flint-gray sky. "Those candles were sold. A customer named Gabe Waters came into the shop and bought them all."

Aunt Joy gave a bark of laughter and Noelle pivoted.

"Gabe Waters came into my shop? He's one of our most famous residents and he's the highest paid stuntman in Hollywood, although lately most of his film work has been shot in Wilmington."

Aunt Joy's face glowed with chirpy interest, which Noelle attributed to her aunt's avid fascination with show business. When her aunt was younger, she'd been featured as an extra in a movie and had talked about the experience for years.

"He was at the bus accident the other night and acted quickly to save a woman who'd fallen down an embankment, and —"

Her aunt stopped Noelle with a sharp smile. "He recently opened an outreach center for disadvantaged youths near the edge of town where he lived when he was a teenager. Gabe's younger cousin hung out with a bad crowd — drugs, alcohol, you name it. That cousin, I believe her name was Holly, was a heap of trouble. Both cousins had neglectful, drug-addicted parents. They were left alone quite often."

Noelle considered the information. "Holly's getting married in Snowing Rock in December. At least, Gabe hopes she is," Noelle clarified. "I helped him select candles for the wedding. Well, mostly Caroline helped. Then he took me to lunch."

Aunt Joy swung her wheelchair round to face Noelle. "He renovated a house in Snowing Rock and is now living there because he dislikes big-city living. Here, he's treated like one of the locals."

"He said he remembered me from high school," Noelle said.

Her aunt sat straighter in her wheelchair, her gaze observant and alert. "He was constantly picked on by bullies because he was a weak, sickly kid. Years ago, I remember someone saying he had a mad crush on you after you stopped a fight between him and—"

"A fight." Noelle hesitated, the remembrances coming back in a rush. When she'd been a freshman, she'd seen two older guys shouting at each other outside a classroom. The bigger guy was pushing and shoving Gabe, jabbing at Gabe's chest with his fingers. Gabe didn't back down, but he didn't throw his fists at the bully, either.

She drew a breath, the words tumbling out. "After I shouted at the guys to stop fighting, Gabe would never meet my gaze in the hallway again."

"He was a senior and probably embarrassed because a freshman girl had protected him in front of his classmates."

Surprise mingled with Noelle's protest. "I hardly protected him. From what I heard, before the end of the school year he'd fought that same bully and won."

"Remember the high school Christmas dance?" Aunt Joy asked.

"Yes." Noelle's recollections circled. "My parents had bought me a red sequined dress. I felt uncomfortable—I didn't know where to stand, where to put my hands. I didn't relate well to my peers because my parents didn't stay in one place long enough. They were always searching for a better piano professor for my lessons and subsequently, I never developed true friendships." Noelle shook her head. "I left the dance early. There was a mistletoe in the doorway and I looked around to be sure no one was watching before I dashed under it and out the nearest exit."

"I was a chaperone and you looked stunning that night. Gabe couldn't take his eyes off you."

Noelle paused, calling to mind the small, thin teen, now a strong, rugged man. "Gabe looks like an actor."

Aunt Joy's eyes gleamed shrewdly. "And most attractive, especially on a big movie screen."

Noelle smiled, envisioning his rough, attractive features.

'I couldn't bear to imagine that I was so forgettable,' he'd said softly.

Her smile wavered. If she had more than a few weeks in Snowing Rock, she might enjoy spending time with him. He was funny and endearing and interesting.

Noelle kissed her aunt on the cheek as she prepared to leave. Her conscience nagged because she was already two days behind in her practice regimen. "Also, Aunt Joy, the damper pedal snapped on your piano. I called a piano technician in Fisher's Crossing."

Aunt Joy sank back in her wheelchair. "No technician will venture up the mountain until the snow subsides, and another storm is predicted within the next couple of days. Have a bite to eat tonight, and rest. Your practice can wait."

Determination fluttered in Noelle's chest. "I'll rest after December fifteenth. My performance must be extraordinary or I'll never be accepted in the concert world again. After what happened last year I'm surprised that Colin forgave—"

"Knowing your ex, he's gaining in some way, probably through increased ticket sales," her aunt interrupted flatly. "And I won't forget how he treated you when you weren't feeling well."

"I had assumed my bloating and nausea were related to exhaustion and stress," Noelle said. "And Colin was either practicing or performing. You know how driven he was, especially after his mother died. Then his father's expectations rose even higher." Noelle shook her head. "I'm sorry I waited so long to see a doctor, because he said my fertility might be decreased. I don't want children yet, but someday ... and if I can't ..."

Noelle paused, remembering the empathy Gabe had shown toward Anjali. Her ex, on the other hand, couldn't tolerate children. They were too noisy and jumpy, he'd declared.

Aunt Joy patted Noelle's hand. "If you slow down, someday you'll have children. If not children of your own, then you can adopt." Her smile was gentle, her tone kindhearted. "Don't let ambition cause you to lose sight of what's really important."

Noelle gazed directly into her aunt's perceptive eyes. "All my parents wanted was for me to succeed. I wasn't there for them when they died, and they were always there for me. I failed them."

"What could you have done differently? You were in a different state when the car crash happened and you arrived at the hospital shortly afterward. Confront your supposed failure, view it as a learning experience, and keep moving forward." Aunt Joy's hand stayed resting on Noelle's. "You're mistaking your parents' ambitions with your own. You'll succeed by not overdoing things."

After quick farewells, Noelle departed for her aunt's cottage. She didn't take time to rest, nor eat, as her aunt had suggested. Instead, Noelle lay on her back, shining her phone's flashlight at the small lever beneath the piano.

She cursed the piano, something she'd never done before, because the lever didn't fit no matter how hard she tried.

And if she couldn't practice, she'd fail. And if she failed a second time, how could she ever show her face on the concert stage again?

CHAPTER 6

On Friday evening, Noelle was able to leave the shop by six o'clock. That hadn't been easy, because closing meant restocking, dusting and mopping, and balancing the shop's tills.

With a relieved sigh, she pulled on her red, wooly gloves and cream-colored jacket, covered her ears with her red wool hat, then trooped four blocks to the Fernandez's two-story house. Snowing Rock reminded her of a make-believe, wintry hamlet, the icy-blue snow reflecting the glow from polished brass street lamps.

She stepped to the entrance of the Fernandez household and rang the front doorbell.

Anjali opened the door and threw her arms around Noelle's waist. "Hi, Miss Noelle! Come on in!" Her child-like enthusiasm was infectious.

"I'm so glad to see you again!" Noelle laughed.

"Mommy's home from the hospital!" Anjali grabbed Noelle's hand and towed her to the living room.

Mrs. Fernandez sat on the couch with a plaster cast on one leg, a pair of crutches set beside the couch.

Noelle hugged Mrs. Fernandez, then handed her a jasmine candle with a red velvet bow.

Mrs. Fernandez opened the candle jar and sniffed. "Thank you. Jasmine's my favorite fragrance. So delicate."

"And Jasmine is supposed to be a good scent for sleeping," Noelle pointed out.

"Who can sleep in this busy house?" Mrs. Fernandez gestured around the living room, littered with an array of plush stuffed animals, a dollhouse, and a ballerina puppet.

A woman strongly resembling Mrs. Fernandez stepped from the kitchen into the room. She had graying hair at the temples, her hair pulled back in a severe bun, accentuating her round cheeks and double chin. She flashed a smile.

"This is Nancy, my sister. She lives next door," Mrs. Fernandez said. "She's assisting me with my Christmas baking orders. I can't get around easily and the doctor said I'll wear this cast another six weeks. Apparently, it takes a while to heal from a broken leg."

Anjali did a cartwheel across the room. "Our house always smells delicious because Mommy and Aunt Nancy bake cookies for everyone in Snowing Rock!"

"Not everyone, Anjali," Aunt Nancy corrected, before swiveling back to the kitchen.

"What's your specialty?" Noelle asked Mrs. Fernandez. "Cakes or cookies?"

Mrs. Fernandez glanced sideways toward the kitchen. "Our plain butter Christmas cookies are very popular. We use powdered sugar, butter, flour, and vanilla."

For a moment, Noelle speculated about asking Mrs. Fernandez if she could offer any tips on baking sugar cookies. That is, until she spotted the upright piano half-hidden behind a pile of blankets in the far corner of the room.

Noelle revolved in a deliberate circle. "You own a piano?"

"Yes. I mentioned on the bus that Anjali's very musical."

For a few minutes, Mrs. Fernandez kept up a one-sided conversation about Snowing Rock's kindergarten choir while Noelle eyed the piano.

"We adopted Anjali from India when she was a baby," Mrs. Fernandez was saying. "My husband wants her to take piano lessons when she gets older."

"Piano lessons will give Anjali the solid foundation she needs to understand music and play other instruments." Noelle edged closer toward the piano. With a spurt of inspiration, she inquired, "May I play your piano? I'm staying at my Aunt Joy's cottage and the pedal on her piano is broken."

Mrs. Fernandez relaxed against the sofa. "Ours is an old player piano. There should be a music roll in the spool box. Pull the lever bar, open the compartment doors, and start pumping the pedals. 'A Holly, Jolly Christmas' is on the spool."

"I don't need to pump the pedals. I'm a professional pianist and I'm preparing for a concert in Saint Augustine next month." Noelle moved the blankets to the side, sat on the bench, and played several octaves.

Nancy appeared at the kitchen doorway with a soapy dish in her hand. "You're a professional piano player? Can you play 'We Need A Little Christmas'? I enjoy hearing music when I'm washing dishes."

Noelle's forehead knit into a frown. Apparently, a serious Chopin etude wasn't the top choice on anyone's play list.

Anjali dashed to the piano. "I can play! Wanna hear, Miss Noelle?" Anjali found the E key and pressed three times. "Jin gle bells, jin gle bells. Isn't that good?"

"Excellent!" Noelle clapped her hands in approval while Anjali gave a triumphant hoot.

"If you need a piano to practice, you're welcome to come over on Sunday afternoons," Mrs. Fernandez said.

"Thanks," Noelle accepted, abandoning the idea of practicing during this visit.

She stood and admired the huge floral arrangement set on the shelf beside the piano, a 'Be Happy' mug bursting with yellow roses.

"The bouquet was delivered yesterday," Mrs. Fernandez remarked. "It's from Mr. Gabe Waters, the famous stuntman. Anjali said he was the first person to come to my aid at the bus accident."

Noelle flicked her gaze upward. Somehow, the conversation had shifted from piano practice to Gabe.

"Yes, he acted swiftly and bravely," Noelle agreed.

"The doctor said that Mr. Waters saved me from developing hypothermia."

Noelle sniffed the sweet fragrance of the roses, and read the hand-written card attached. 'I wanted to brighten your home and your spirits. Wishing you a speedy recovery. Gabe.'

In fairness, he was generous and considerate. And he hadn't hesitated in risking his life to rescue Mrs. Fernandez.

"He also sent dinner last night from the sub shop on Main Street," Mrs. Fernandez finished.

Anjali twirled around the living room and landed on the floor beside her mother. "I love subs! How did Mr. Gabe know my favorite sub was wheat bread with banana peppers and turkey? He's a super-hero and can read minds!"

"Anjali, Mr. Waters called me to find out your favorite sub ahead of time," Mrs. Fernandez clarified.

Anjali rubbed her eyes. "Do superheroes always win, Miss Noelle?"

"Always," Noelle said emphatically.

The little girl tilted her head. "Then Mommy's right and Mr. Gabe's not a super-hero. Wanna hear how I know?"

"Absolutely!" Noelle lowered her gaze and hid her laugh.

Anjali's almond eyes gleamed. "Mr. Gabe played checkers with me in the hospital and he couldn't beat me. Not once, although he said he really, really tried." Anjali embellished her deduction with another twirl.

Noelle smiled. She had to admit that Gabe was pretty great, even if he wasn't a superhero.

CHAPTER 7

Noelle rushed into the candle shop at nine on Saturday morning wielding a tray of homemade sugar cookies. Admittedly. some of the cookies were doughy because she hadn't waited for the oven to pre-heat, although she'd been able to salvage two dozen. The rest of the cookies had been burned beyond recognition because she'd forgotten about them as she'd tried to fix the piano's damper pedal.

She'd been unsuccessful, and silent piano practice wasn't going well.

A shriek of cold wind helped blow the candle shop's door open. She shook her tingling fingertips and changed into flat, red shoes to offset her black leggings. Then she pulled off her light gray wool scarf, winter wool hat, and smoothed her red tunic sweater to her wrists.

Her body shivered while she thawed out and admired the glow of lit candles placed around the shop, sifting scents of eucalyptus, cranberry, and Fraser pine through the air.

"Good morning, Miss Saint Augustine," Caroline greeted Noelle with her usual happy grin. She stood behind the cash register and flipped a turquoise skinny braid behind her ear. "Those cookies look good."

"Thanks." Noelle stepped to the back room, hung her coat, and placed the sugar cookies on the counter. "Last night, I ate a dozen that burned and I'm still on a sugar rush. If I keep eating at this rate, I won't be able to fit into my black formal gown for my piano performance."

"You're tall and trim and will look dazzling in a long black gown. Besides, calories don't count if the cookies are burned." Caroline laughed, then grew serious. "We've received an order for ten vanilla scented beeswax votive candles this morning from Mr. Waters."

"I thought he wanted Candleglow and Mistletoe candles for his cousin's wedding?"

"Apparently, he wants beeswax candles, too."

"Do we have any in stock?" Noelle asked.

"A few. I placed an order this morning for the additional candles, and they should arrive well before the wedding."

An hour later, Noelle realized that the time had passed in a blur. Polar-white snow battering against the shop's front window hadn't deterred the enthusiastic candle shoppers.

"I wish our candle-making class started earlier tonight, don't you, Noelle?" Caroline prompted when the endless stream of customers had slowed.

Noelle would've rather wished for her aunt's piano to have a working damper pedal, although she didn't want to confide that wish to Caroline and deflate Caroline's enthusiasm.

"I've never made a candle before, remember?" Noelle softened her response with a kindly smile.

"You'll love it! And I'm available as long as you need me tonight because Alan is working at the pizzeria until midnight."

"Your relationship with Alan seems to be getting serious. With your math skills, I thought you wanted to open a successful office and marry a New York banker?"

Caroline shrugged. "Alan's a nice guy and treats me like a princess." She beamed a welcoming smile to two customers entering the shop. "Welcome to 'Scents of Joy'!"

In spite of Caroline's endless exuberance, Noelle rubbed her forehead. It didn't take a genius to realize that Saturday was going to be a very long day.

NOELLE CLOSED the candle shop at six, placing a sign in the window to remind customers the candle-making class began at seven. Outside, battering gusts blew the street lights back and forth, and people held their coats close against them as they battled the onslaught of the wind.

Noelle had an hour to cash out and clean before organizing the supplies for the candle-making class. She made her way to the shop's tiny bathroom and wrung out several paper towels, pressing them against her forehead as a cold pack to refresh herself. She washed her face in the small sideways sink, then applied a dab of rose blush and red lip gloss.

She was tired and hungry. Surely her waistline would forgive her if she ate one tiny, doughy, sugar cookie? She was still debating when she wandered to the front of the shop and peered out the window. The snow was falling hard and heavy, and occasionally a screech of wind rose up, then died down.

At six forty-five, a line of customers had formed. Winter had filled the streets and a pale moon hung high in the sky. It had stopped snowing and the clouds had moved on.

Caroline draped two long tables with plastic tablecloths and covered the tables with newspaper. Small mason jars, glass measuring cups, scissors, roughly chopped beeswax, and wicks sat in the center of each table. On a side counter, she'd plugged in a dozen crock pots in a row of extension cords. Several old washcloths were placed alongside for clean-up.

"There are supplies for at least a dozen people." Caroline lit several beeswax candles and placed them on the table, then veered to Noelle. "Can you get the sugar cookies and make hot chocolate? I'm using a mix, so stir in boiling water."

"Sure." With a plan to eat at least three cookies, Noelle walked down the hallway to the storage room, stopping in mid-step when a large boom rattled the building. All the lights in the candle shop went out simultaneously and the hallway went black. She gripped a corner of the wall and looked around.

"Hey! You okay?" Caroline hurried toward Noelle carrying a stubby, lit candle. "A transformer must've blown because of the weight of the snow. Let's test all the fuses in the breaker panel and switch on the generator. I let the customers inside and invited them to find a seat."

After checking all the switches, they started the generator. The light in the shop would be low, but efficient. When they returned to the front, a half dozen women were seated at one table. From the corner of her eye, Noelle noted that a handsome man was seated at the second table.

"Hi, Noelle." Gabe stood and shrugged off his olive green parka.

His hazel eyes gleamed, his wavy chestnut hair wet with snow. He looked super attractive in dark, slim jeans and a cream-colored wool sweater hugging his sculpted shoulders.

"Gabe?" she asked blankly. "What are you doing at a candle class?"

"I've been at my outreach center since dawn. I was driving by the candle shop on my way home and saw the lights go out. I thought you might need some help." His gaze drifted appreciatively over her clingy, red tunic sweater. His admiring appraisal made her pulse quicken and she attributed her reaction to relief, knowing his capable presence could fix any problem if another should arise.

She extended her hands. "Thanks for stopping by. Caroline and I were able to figure out the generator."

He held her hands in his. "I called the power company and the estimated repair time is four hours." He glanced good-naturedly at the candles arranged on the tables. "You're definitely in the right business for this town."

"Snowing Rock might be good business for candles, although it's not so good for pianists who need to practice." Noelle surveyed the darkened shop and cash register and an appealing idea occurred. Without electricity, she wouldn't be able to ring up any supplies, therefore, she couldn't offer the candle-making class. Elation hummed through her veins. She could head back to her aunt's cottage to practice.

She dropped her hands from his. "Because of the power outage, we'll need to reschedule the class for next Saturday evening," she announced, amidst groans of dismay from the ladies. "Please help yourself to the sugar cookies I baked before you leave. Have a safe drive—"

"Nonsense. You're all welcome to stay!" Caroline interrupted, oozing with enthusiasm. "There's candle power and enough electricity so the crock pots will melt the beeswax."

The ladies seated at the opposite table applauded their approval.

"And I'll pay for all the supplies." Gabe tipped his head toward the cash register, then back to Noelle. He winked. "You can add the cost to my wedding bill."

Noelle opened her mouth to sputter an objection and he lightly placed his finger on her lips. "As we say in the acting business, the show must go on. To repay my kindness, all I want is a sugar cookie in return."

Pivoting on her heel, Noelle grabbed some cookies and napkins, tramped back to her seat, and handed him two cookies.

"Thanks." His lips twitched. "Have you ever made a candle, by the way?"

"Never. Have you?"

"No, but I'm willing to learn and I'm certain you're an excellent teacher."

One look at his joking grin and Noelle half-sighed. "I'm a pianist. I'm not qualified to teach this class."

"I am, though, Miss Saint Augustine." Tying a fresh white apron around her thick waist, Caroline called for attention. "In the center of the table are small-mouthed mason jars and #4 cotton square braided wicks." Caroline held up a mason jar. "Joy and I found that a fifty/fifty blend of palm oil mixed with beeswax will produce beautiful candles."

"Why palm oil?" Noelle asked.

"Because palm oil is softer, with a low melt point." Caroline grabbed some beeswax, measured twelve ounces in a glass measuring cup, then encouraged the class to do the same. "The crock pots are set on low and will allow the beeswax to melt slowly."

Noelle smiled. The brilliant math senior with the ever-changing hair color and merry demeanor spoke passionately about candle making and, consequently, made the topic interesting.

"While we're waiting, we'll waltz back to the table to measure and cut our wicks." Caroline held a fistful of wicks in her hand and danced back to the table. "Then we'll dip the wicks into the melted wax."

Gabe rested his arm on the back of Noelle's seat, his hand brushing against her shoulder.

"May I suggest the longer wick to your right?" He stretched his legs beneath the table, his hard muscles pressing intimately against hers.

She took a bite of the second sugar cookie he hadn't touched and leaned back, feeling content. "After one class you think you know more about making candles than I do, I presume?"

He chuckled. Reaching around her for the wick, his hand touched hers, his gaze drifting to her face. "I'd say we're equals."

He really was the most provoking man she'd ever met, she mused with a grin. "And I'd say that I'm the boss," she said.

They were so close, his face stopped within an inch of hers, his warm breath glancing over her cheeks as he tipped her chin up to meet his hazel eyes. "Whatever you say, boss."

AN HOUR LATER, Noelle stood to admire her and Gabe's candles. He'd touched and brushed against her so much during the lesson, she almost didn't care that she'd missed precious piano practice time.

Her gaze met his. They'd poured in palm oil when the beeswax was completely melted and stirred each other's wax with a skewer.

"Caroline's instructions were to pour only one half inch of wax in the jar. However, I'll hold your wick in place if you'll hold mine," he said. "You'll notice that my wick is standing up on its own."

Noelle gulped back an exasperated laugh at his sensual insinuation. "So we're both officially candle makers." She poured the remaining hot wax into his jar, then hers, leaving a space at the top in order for the wax to harden.

He nodded toward a row of lit beeswax candles set in the middle of the table and grinned roguishly. "You're beautiful by candlelight, Noelle. Red suits you."

"Always the charmer, Gabe." She felt herself flush, caught in the spell of his persuasive gaze. She offered a bright smile, submitting to his attraction, admitting to herself that she truly enjoyed being with him.

She looked around, taking in the empty shop. She and Gabe had been so absorbed with each other that she hadn't realized a couple of hours had sped by and all the customers had left.

His white teeth flashed an indulgent, slow smile. "I learned a new skill tonight."

Her gaze fell to the lively flickers of burning candles, the scents of honey warming the air. "Yes, it was fun."

Lightly, he pushed her hair back and touched her forehead. "Your bruise is gone."

"Bruise?" With awkward hands, she tried to restore order to her hair. "I'd forgotten about it."

He slipped his arm around her and pushed a wayward curl from her face. "Caroline said my candle is a bright, sunny yellow. How about yours?"

Noelle laughed aloud, realizing that since she'd sat beside him this evening, she hadn't fretted about her upcoming performance or her practice schedule.

"Caroline said that my candle hardened back to its original beeswax shade, which is the color it should be," she admonished him with a laugh.

His eyes were warm, a deep golden, the color of beeswax honey.

His gaze darkened. Unhurriedly, he bent his head and she knew he was going to kiss her.

She didn't resist, gazing up at the attractive man who offered her gentleness and affection. His lips came down to caress hers in a tender, unhurried kiss. His arms wrapped around her, pulling her closer. She closed her eyes and touched a hand to his sculpted chest.

Caroline cleared her throat. "Well, you two," she interrupted, bringing Noelle plummeting back to the reality of the candle shop.

Noelle stepped away from Gabe, feeling her ears heat, most likely to a bright red. Caroline had strolled over just in time to observe their quickly broken kiss.

Attached to her cell phone, Caroline continued, "Alan's getting out of the pizzeria early and treating me to a late-night date."

"Go have fun, Caroline," Noelle said. "I'll clean the shop. You deserve extra pay for all you do."

"You're not getting paid, either," Caroline reminded. "Your aunt said you're refusing the weekly salary she offered you."

Gabe's gaze shifted to the crock pots, discarded wicks, and strewn scissors. "And I won't let you to clean this shop by yourself, Noelle."

"I don't need any help." Noelle hesitated and took a long breath. Yes she did, if she wanted to retreat to her aunt's cottage and practice all thirty-six major and minor scales before midnight.

A fierce blast of wintry wind blew into the shop as a college-aged man strode in. His hair stood straight up in a military buzz cut and several piercings gleamed from his ears. His protruding nose was a deep, dark red, resembling the color of merlot wine.

Caroline tossed a glance toward him and her lips parted. "Hi Alan. This is Noelle and Mr. Gabe Waters."

"Hi everyone," Alan nodded. "And hi, hot stuff." Alan blew Caroline an air kiss while holding up a pizza box and bottle of water. "Anyone like pizza?"

"Thanks, I'm famished," Noelle said. Mentally, a part of her tried to calculate how long it would take to eat a few pizza slices so that she could get back to her aunt's cottage and practice.

She stole a glance at Gabe's expectant, smiling expression, his handsome face. The other part of her acknowledged that she wanted to share a few extra minutes with him.

"The candle wax is easier to clean once it's hardened, and the newspaper should've caught most of the spills," Caroline was explaining to Gabe. "If you wash the crock pots, remember not to pour any of the water down the drain. I've clogged the drain a couple of times because there's always some melted wax left at the bottom of the pot."

After quick goodbyes to Caroline and Alan, Gabe grabbed an armload of paper towels and headed for the storage room. "I'll take these supplies and check on the generator, Noelle. Then we'll eat, all right?"

Noelle gathered wicks and empty jars. She eyed the empty cookie tray, feeling shaky and exhausted. She quickened her pace past the crock pots on the shelf and caught her foot on an extension cord. She tripped, bracing her right arm on the shelf to stop her fall while the wicks and empty jars clattered to the floor. The crock pot overturned, and a blinding pain seared through her as hot, melted wax poured across the back of her right hand.

She gasped aloud and stared at her burning hand. How could she practice piano? How would she perform at her concert? She froze, the air bursting in and out of her lungs.

"Noelle!" Gabe appeared in an instant. "What happened?"

Hastily, she wiped the tears coursing down her cheeks. "I tripped on the crock pot cords. I was rushing. I should've been paying closer attention."

"Don't be so hard on yourself. Those cords aren't usually there and were easy to miss." He examined her hand, steered her to the bathroom, and ran the cold water. "Looks like a first-degree burn, although it's too early to determine yet. Leave your hand beneath the water. I'll get my Land Rover and take you to the hospital."

Noelle complied, gasping at the stinging spray of cold water cutting into her hand as a knifelike burn. She tried to pull her hand away. "Please, Gabe. No hospitals."

"All right, I'll take you to your aunt's cottage." His expression changed from worry to acquiescence. Carefully, he rolled up the sleeves of her tunic. "You don't want your sleeves getting wet and changing to icicles."

"We can't leave Aunt Joy's shop such a mess." Nervously, Noelle fingered the hem of her tunic with her left hand. "The shop isn't cleaned and my aunt's very fussy—"

"I'll clean the shop later." Gabe stroked the hair from Noelle's forehead in a slow, soothing motion. His gesture made her tears flow harder, and he withdrew a clean white handkerchief from his pocket and wiped her cheeks.

"Keep your hand beneath the cold water while I get my Land Rover, all right?" He shrugged on his parka and grabbed the pizza box and water on his way out.

A few minutes later, he strode through the shop's entry and stamped the snow from his black work boots. He shut off the bathroom faucet, extinguished the beeswax candles, and helped her put on her boots, hat and coat.

Bleakly, she stared out the candle shop's front window, feeling imprisoned by a winter-white specter of glaring snow and naked trees. She dried her eyes once more with his proffered cotton handkerchief, thankful that her last gush of tears had eased. Ruefully, she shook her head. "Please, I can manage, Gabe."

"You don't have to be brave for me, Noelle," he said quietly.

She searched his face, seeing kindness and compassion etched on his strong features. "I'm too much of a bother."

He kept one arm around her and led her to the shop's entrance. "You'll never be a bother to me, all right?"

Briefly, she closed her eyes to will away the burning pain as she watched his tall frame trudge through the snow to open the passenger door, then hurry back to assist her.

He needed a shave. He'd admitted he'd been at his outreach center since dawn.

Yet he was concerned and endearing, never complaining nor asking anything in return. She didn't need to prove anything to him.

She handed him the keys to the candle shop and he assisted her into his Land Rover.

With a quiet exhale, she sank back into the comfortable leather seat and closed her eyes. Perhaps just this once, she'd rely on someone else, trust someone else. Just this once.

CHAPTER 8

G abe watched Noelle's tight expression as he drove the short distance to her aunt's cottage. The streets were tomblike, dark and silent, the power still out. He parked in front of 10 Oak Street, slid out of the driver seat and used his cell phone's flashlight to guide Noelle inside.

The cottage was a single-storied house, cozy and old-fashioned. A snow shovel sat by the front door, and a woodsy fir tree scent lingered in the hallway as they entered the living room. Two Candleglow and Mistletoe candles, along with old, twisted matches, sat on the coffee table.

Logs and kindling were neatly stacked beside the ceramic, wood-burning fireplace.

He flicked on the light switch for when the electricity would be restored, then helped Noelle take off her jacket and boots. He steered her to the flowered couch, setting a red crocheted blanket to one side. He placed the pizza on a nearby table and lit the candles.

The cheery warmth flooded the room.

Noting Noelle's slumped posture, he said calmly, "Let me see your hand again."

She held out her hand. "How bad? Tell me the truth."

"The burn site is swollen and red," he said. "Is it painful?"

"It stings." She frowned, then ventured guardedly. "Why?"

"Because the blister hasn't swelled nor opened." Carefully, he pressed on the burn and she winced. "The blisters whitened and that's a good sign. So far, the burn looks first-degree. Still, it can get worse and change to second-degree without warning."

"How long before it changes? Then what?"

"If the burn becomes red and shiny and swells more, we'll decide what to do next."

Her gaze flitted around the room. She fidgeted with the sleeves of her tunic sweater. "What if I can't practice? If I miss a day, my technique will suffer. I'll be in the limelight in Saint Augustine, and my performance must be perfect, without a mistake."

Gabe started for the kitchen. "Don't worry about practicing now. Sit back and I'll get a bowl of cold water."

"Should you add ice?" Her voice choked with tears. "I thought I'd read—"

As compassionately as he could, Gabe answered, "Ice causes frostbite and might damage your skin. Cold water will pull the heat away." He rummaged through the wooden cabinets in the tidy kitchen, surprisingly modern considering the rustic, stone exterior of the cottage.

He opened the stainless-steel refrigerator, relieved to find orange juice, because he felt a drop in his sugar levels imminent. He quickly checked his levels, found them low, then poured himself a glass of orange juice. Fortunately, they'd be eating pizza within fifteen minutes.

He tried to take good care of himself, managing his diabetes by watching his diet and staying physically fit, although sometimes he got sidetracked.

While he filled a bowl on the counter with cold water, he blew out a breath. He was sidetracked all right, by power outages and candle-making classes and a beautiful, distressed blonde.

He returned to the living room to find that very same blonde curled up on the couch, blowing on her hand. Her hair fell in wisps around her heart-shaped face and she lifted her long, graceful fingers to push a strand behind her ear. Despite her lackluster movements, she presented such an entrancing image by candlelight that he forced himself to shove back the urge to pull her onto his lap and comfort her. Instead, he shifted and set the bowl of cold water on the coffee table.

"Put your hand in the water," he said. "And blowing on the burn doesn't help. In fact, it can lead to infection. Any chance your aunt keeps antibiotic cream and gauze and Ibuprofen in her medicine cabinet?"

"Probably, knowing how meticulous Aunt Joy is," Noelle replied.

He was already striding out of the room. He came back with some Ibuprofen tablets, glasses and two turquoise ceramic plates from the kitchen, along with antibiotic cream and gauze.

"I'll serve pizza first and then you can take Ibuprofen to head off the pain." He studied Noelle's complexion, devoid of color, and frowned. "When was the last time you ate?"

She half-smiled. "Do burned cookies from last night count?"

"No. Eat a slice of pizza, then take the Ibuprofen."

Her gaze narrowed briefly. "Can I remove my hand from the cold water?"

"Yes." He went to the bathroom sink and washed his hands, returned to the living room with a hand towel, and dried her wound. Then, he applied antibiotic cream, gauze, and a bandage.

"The power and heat should be back on soon," he said. "In the meantime, I'll light a fire in the fireplace."

Using the dry wood and kindling and old twisted matches, a cozy fire soon spat at them.

A few minutes later, some color had touched her face, and her cheeks had pinkened.

"I like cold pizza," she said.

"I do, too." He poured water into their glasses and raised his glass. "A toast to cold pizza and warm fireplaces." He added a conspiratorial wink.

"And candlelight."

"And Candleglow and Mistletoe candles," he said.

She gave a thumbs-up with her left hand, then picked up her glass. She broke into a smile and they clinked glasses.

He gazed appreciatively over her slim form. Her attractiveness and feminine allure had prompted many high school guys to stop and stare, doing things, trying to impress her. She'd brushed them all off.

He sat beside her on the couch and patted his arm, signaling for her to lean against him. "You must be exhausted. I'll stay awhile and monitor your burn."

She stared fixedly at the bluish-orange flames of the fire and didn't answer.

He swept his arm around her. "All right?"

She nodded and leaned closer. "I've wanted to light a fire in the fireplace all week, but I'm so weighed down by all the responsibilities of running the shop. I don't have a moment to think and when I get back to the cottage at night it's so late and I'm tired and ..." She swallowed.

"Sometimes, life doesn't go the way we planned," he said softly.

She tipped her head up. "And you weren't always a stuntman."

He offered a non-committal nod. He'd needed to overcome his diabetes and build up his physique in order to fight all the bullies who'd picked on him. He'd been a skinny guy from the poorest section of town who'd learned to become self-reliant in order to survive.

Gabe dropped his arm from her shoulders, leaned forward on the couch, and fingered the rim of his water glass. "Life took me in a different direction," he said.

She examined the bandage and furrowed her brow. "I should be grateful the burn is on the back of my right hand. I'm left-handed. At least I can still eat."

He set down his glass and turned to her, gently running his forefinger across her high cheekbone. He'd always admired her dedication and perseverance. She was everything he'd remembered, fresh, vivacious, and astonishingly fearless despite her fragile outward appearance.

"You inspired me to succeed, did you know that?" he asked.

She waved a flippant hand at herself and leaned back. "Me? Hardly. Your success is your own and you should claim it. I've heard that you're the highest paid stuntman in the business and in great demand."

"And you've made a celebrated name for yourself in the music world." He observed the piano in the corner of the living room. "So this is the piano you're practicing on for your performance?"

Her lovely mouth downturned. "Yes, except the piano doesn't work. The damper pedal broke and I don't know how to repair it, so I'm practicing silently without touching the keys. Although when I visited Mrs. Fernandez the other day, I discovered she owns an upright player piano." Noelle licked her lips, her posture stiffened. "She said I can practice at her house on Sunday afternoons. In the meantime, I'll read more about Chopin's style. That type of knowledge helps me connect with the composer."

"Sounds like an agreeable solution," Gabe surmised.

"I should be resigned to scrambling for a piano because I've never actually had one since living in an apartment. In Saint Augustine, Colin and I practiced at the university because we both taught music theory classes there part-time. Pianos and apartment high-rises don't go together. The neighbors would complain about the noise."

"I'm still getting over the fact that a concert pianist doesn't own a piano." Gabe brushed his fingers along her neck, up to her temple.

Noelle shivered and gave a small smile. "I inherited a beautiful baby grand piano in an ebony, glossy finish from my parents. They'd engraved my initials, N.W., inside the fallboard, and I kept all my old sheet music inside the matching bench. They settled in a suburb outside New York City after I moved to Saint Augustine. And then, they died unexpectedly in a car accident. My terrible performance occurred one month later." She rubbed her legs with her uninjured hand, and tears spilled from her sea-green eyes. "I avoided everyone afterward. I've just gone back to playing a few months ago."

Gabe offered her shoulders a comforting squeeze and murmured in her ear. "Why was your performance a disaster, Noelle?"

As if an interval of several minutes hadn't ticked by, she replied, "I wasn't concentrating and, consequently, suffered a memory lapse. I panicked and dashed off the stage. Colin was furious because we were performing a duo-piano concert and he couldn't finish the piece without me, and his father was watching. Colin's father is his worst critic." Noelle sighed and shrugged. "Anyway, Colin recovered brilliantly and performed a showy Liszt piano solo as a finale. He served me with divorce papers the following day and told me I was inept and didn't deserve happiness after what I'd done."

"For dashing off the stage?"

"Our marital problems had begun long before that particular performance. He was brought up by a nanny after his mother died, and his father only paid attention to Colin when Colin played flawlessly. Consequently, Colin was more interested in his performances than in me."

"You were always poised and professional."

"Not always. I cried so hard afterward because he was my husband and wasn't supposed to let me down. I had faith he would be there for me. When I confronted him, he said I was insecure and a coward."

She stared at the long shadows the fire in the fireplace had created across the woven wool rug. The fiery glow had gilded her blonde hair to shiny gold. She looked incredibly attractive in that soft red sweater, like a living flame, pure and vibrant.

"When I knew you in high school ..." he said.

She shook her head. "That teenage girl you knew was young and naive and didn't realize the hard road ahead of her. When you met me, I was a freshman. I was too cocky, too sure of myself. I soon discovered that music critics are merciless."

He pulled her closer. "And so was your ex," he said.

"Sometimes I don't believe I deserve a second chance after how poorly I performed."

"You deserve the world," Gabe said.

Something inside his chest squeezed. Despite the way she'd explained her poor performance by blaming herself, the aftermath had left her hurt and susceptible. She'd admitted her lack of trust in people. Yet, this brave, beautiful woman had summoned up the courage to return to the concert stage, the spotlight of her humiliation.

The tender affection Gabe felt for her multiplied. For the first time, he realized how devastated she must've felt after all her years of hard work and endless preparation. Her ex, as well as the critics, had been thoughtless and mean-spirited. And Gabe would've happily tossed the lot of them into the street and left them there.

Outwardly calm, Gabe said nothing. He lifted his glass and drained the water that was left. As she'd once protected him, he decided, he'd protect her from anyone who'd try to hurt her.

Noelle pulled from his arms and straightened. "Colin's given me an opportunity to redeem myself on December fifteenth at the Forum Theater."

Impatiently, Gabe fiddled with the sleeves of his wool sweater. "Somehow, I think Colin will benefit in some way."

"I've had reservations, too, although my need to prove myself outweighs my fear of exploitation. It's a professional gig and I'll be paid." She blew out a breath. "My performance will be a success, and then Christmas will be special again."

Gabe took her cold fingers in his. "Christmas isn't dependent on a piano performance. Christmas is about being surrounded by special friends and loved ones."

And cold pizza and glowing candles and a spirited, gutsy woman, he thought.

Her head bowed. "I haven't enjoyed a happy Christmas in a while. This town ... I'd forgotten how wonderful the holiday festivities were, the snow, the joyful decorations, although it's not even Thanksgiving yet."

"How's Christmas in Saint Augustine?" he asked.

She drew a long breath, then blew it out. "Lonely."

He considered her for a long, silent minute. Not this Christmas, he vowed.

"My parents talked about taking me to the O'Donnell farm for a sleigh ride, then cutting down a Christmas tree, although we never did. They were the scholarly type and weren't interested in outdoor activities. From the advertisements, I always admired the property."

Slowly, Gabe nodded. "I know that farm well."

Her green-eyed gaze widened. "Is the farm still open after all these years?"

"The farm opens Thanksgiving evening," he replied dryly.

"Do you know the owner?"

"Intimately."

He'd surprise her, Gabe decided with an inward smile. He'd bought the farm five years ago when he'd decided to make Snowing Rock his permanent residence. He, too, had admired the farm before it had fallen into disrepair. He'd purchased and renovated the house, barns, and rambling ten acres. His thriftiness during his lean years had paid off.

He couldn't help imagining the two of them running the farm together.

AN HOUR WENT BY, the fire had waned to silvery ashes, and Noelle slept soundly against his arm. Gently, he roused her. "I'll be leaving soon and will change your bandage. Is there anything else you need?"

With her eyes still closed, she mumbled, "No."

He placed several comfortable throw pillows beneath her head, covered her with the crocheted blanket, and placed a tender kiss on her forehead. She looked fragile and vulnerable, and he wanted to kiss away the remaining tension from her face.

This holiday season would be magical for her.

"Do you want to go on a sleigh ride with me?" he whispered.

"I won't have time." Her eyes remained closed. "I have to spend every minute ..."

"Practicing," he finished.

Carefully, he unwound the gauze to check the wound one more time.

Scarcely believing what he saw, his heart dropped.

CHAPTER 9

"Noelle, wake up."

Shaken by a sense of prickling alarm because of the tenseness in Gabe's voice, Noelle's eyes snapped open. She stared down at the stinging, unbandaged wound on her hand with horror.

She half-rose from the couch. "The burn changed to second-degree? How?"

Gabe's hand tightened on her fingers. "The burn's blistering, however, it's less than three inches, so won't require medical attention."

Slightly, she rocked back and forth. "How long will a second-degree burn take to heal?"

"First-degree burns usually heal in three to six days. Second-degree will take days longer." He cupped her chin in his hands and forced her to meet his gaze. "Either way, I promise you'll be all right."

She felt her cheeks warm. Her panic was unreasonable when he spoke so encouragingly. The burn would heal. Despite her doubts, Gabe had known what to do. He seemed capable of handling any emergency.

"I'll get a fresh bandage." He stepped to the bathroom to wash his hands and returned, applying antibiotic ointment and rewrapping her burn in clean gauze and a bandage. Then he carried their empty plates and pizza box to the kitchen.

Suddenly, the lights flashed on with a hum, and Noelle blinked at the unexpected glare of the overhead living room light.

"Hurray, the power's restored!" Gabe called from the kitchen. "I'll reset the microwave and oven clocks."

In the overhead light, Noelle noticed hard slivers of candle wax, as well as spilled pizza sauce, clinging to her tunic and leggings.

"I should change," she said, half to herself. She stretched out her legs and blew out the candles.

Gabe peered through the kitchen doorway. "Go ahead. I'm almost finished here."

She padded to the bedroom. Slowly and with effort, she slipped out of her clothes and pulled on a slightly frayed pink cashmere lounge suit. The lounge suit was warm and soft, an investment piece from years earlier when she could justify the expense.

She studied her bandaged hand. How was she expected to perform in a piano concert successfully when she couldn't even change her clothes with ease? With a heavy sigh, she headed back toward the living room.

"For a damsel in distress, you look lovely." Gabe's voice checked her in mid-step. He still stood in the middle of the kitchen with a dish towel over his shoulder, the sleeves of his sweater rolled up to expose sculpted arms and a tattoo on his right forearm.

"I like a man who does the dishes." She came closer, reading the words on his tattoo. "'Running away from your problems is a race you'll never win.'"

"Words to live by," he said. "And I was drawn to the snowy mountain background."

She smiled resignedly. "I've always wanted a tattoo with meaningful words, although I was never brave enough to get one. Besides, my ex wouldn't allow it. He controlled my career, what I wore on stage, how low I should bow after a finale, and how many seconds I should wait before coming back onstage after a standing ovation."

"Your ex was a brainless idiot, and you're the most courageous woman I've ever known. You're being proactive by accepting his invitation and proving your resourcefulness." Gabe's admiring gaze slid the length of her body and a faint smile touched his lips. Slowly, he set the dish towel next to the sink and strode to her.

"Will you allow me one parting kiss to remember an adventurous evening?" he asked.

She drew a ragged breath and he brought her to his chest, kissing her long and lingering on the lips. She slid her fingers beneath the wavy hair at his nape, her heart beating in slow, unsteady lurches. An eternity later, he lifted his lips from hers and framed her face in his hands. "Let's exchange cell phone numbers and then I'll leave. You must be exhausted."

She nodded and quickly retrieved her cell phone. He typed in her number and sent her a text. 'You are unbelievably beautiful.'

"Are you trying to make me blush?"

"I'm stating the obvious truth. Now get some sleep." He pressed a kiss on her forehead and shrugged into his parka. In a tone that brooked no disagreement, he added, "If you need anything tonight, call me, all right?"

"I will."

Soon afterward, Noelle went to bed. She heard Gabe shoveling the outside walk, and she smiled. That was just like him, thinking of everyone and everything except himself.

She lay on her back and lifted her bandaged hand, staring at the bandage in the darkness, confident the burn would heal as quickly as Gabe predicted.

She buried herself beneath the blankets, trying to understand the rush of emotions he aroused in her. She didn't have time for a romantic relationship, she reminded herself, because she was resolved to practice diligently, then return to Saint Augustine and perform brilliantly. Nothing would change that.

Yet, all her thoughts drifted back to Gabe.

Because he was proving to be trustworthy and honorable. Because she enjoyed his company. Because when he was near, she felt protected and safe.

Through the lace bedroom curtains, she watched the polar-white snow falling softly to the ground. The frosty November moon was high overhead peeking through the clouds, and shiny icicles had formed on the window casing. Snowing Rock had remained the enchanting Christmas town she'd remembered from her youth.

Perhaps when her concert was over, she could return and finally put down roots, making this charming town her home. Her aunt would need more help as Christmas neared. Plus, Gabe lived here.

His humor was witty, his manner compelling. For the first time in several years, she was looking forward to Christmas. Despite her leeriness of attachments, it was alarming how easily she could picture herself making a life in Snowing Rock.

She sank deeper under the covers, planning every detail of the holiday.

First, a sleigh ride at the O'Donnell farm. She envisioned a majestic, spotted draft horse

116

pulling a sleigh while she admired a breathtaking snowscape. She'd snuggle beneath a plaid wool blanket and inhale crisp mountain air. She'd be cozying up to Gabe, his body warm next to hers, the sound of sleigh bells and their laughter ringing in the air. The day would be picture perfect.

Noelle rolled to her side, reluctant to surrender those heart-warming thoughts as she fell into a groggy sleep.

One more thought made her eyes snap open. She stared at the empty shadows.

She was wary about allowing anyone to get too close. The wall she'd put up after her parents' deaths and her disastrous concert was one of self-preservation, tidily protecting herself from becoming too vulnerable.

Should she let down her guard, take a risk, and truly trust Gabe?

CHAPTER 10

Noelle blinked at the bright, wintry sun streaming through the bedroom window and rubbed her eyes. Her cell phone rang insistently on the night table beside the bed.

She picked up the phone, noting Gabe's name on the caller ID. "Hello?"

"Good morning, gorgeous. I'm cleaning your aunt's shop, then shoveling her walkway. How are you feeling?" he asked.

She glanced at the clock on the night table and gasped at the time, past ten o'clock. Although she wasn't a morning person, she'd never slept this late.

She studied her bandaged hand with frustration, the previous night's memories flashing through her mind. "I feel tired and the burn stings," she confessed.

"Can you be ready in about two hours? I'll bring a late breakfast, change your bandages, then we'll go to the Fernandez's house. If you're up to practicing, I can discuss my cousin's wedding cake details with Mrs. Fernandez."

Noelle envisioned the bustling Fernandez household, wondering how she'd ever be able to concentrate on refining her piano pieces, especially using one hand, and with Gabe in the room.

"I'll entertain Anjali," he continued, as if reading Noelle's thoughts. "All right?"

She nodded into the phone, ended the call, then quickly called Aunt Joy and explained the events of the previous evening. Noelle ended with the reassurance that she was receiving excellent care from Gabe and that her burn should heal within a couple weeks.

Two hours later, the doorbell rang.

"Come in, the door's unlocked," Noelle greeted Gabe as he strode through the doorway. Dressed in his olive green parka and snug-fitting dark jeans, he looked so vital, so good-looking

119

that she favored him with a gaze of appreciation that spanned the length of his athletic body.

Carrying a fast food take-out bag, his gaze drifted from her bandaged hand to her lips. "Does the burn sting?" he asked.

"A little."

"This'll make it better." His mouth descended on hers for a brief kiss.

He kept one arm around her and they walked into the kitchen. He set a corn tortilla filled with cheesy scrambled eggs on the table, along with steaming coffee. "High calorie, high protein diet from the nearest drive-thru restaurant will help you heal quickly. And a cup of coffee so you won't be tired."

She muffled a giggle and sipped her coffee while she stared at him, happily anticipating the upcoming Thanksgiving and sleigh ride they'd enjoy together.

After they'd eaten, he washed his hands with soap and water and unwrapped her old bandage. The wound hadn't gotten worse, and she watched, silently, allowing relief to sink in. He washed his hands a second time, wrapped her hand securely in dry gauze, and taped on a fresh bandage.

The sharp coldness of winter air bit into Noelle's cheeks as she and Gabe headed for his Land Rover. Within minutes, they approached the entrance to the Fernandez home and tapped on the door.

Anjali flung open the door. "Mommy! It's Mr. Gabe and Miss Noelle!"

"Come in!" Mrs. Fernandez, using crutches, crossed the living room and stared at Noelle's bandage. "Mr. Waters told me about your hand when he called this morning. I'm so sorry."

"I needed more practice with my left hand, anyway." Noelle shifted her gaze to the piano. "May I?" She stepped to the piano bench and sat, taking a quick look toward Mrs. Fernandez who bobbed her consent.

Anjali bound to the piano. "Miss Noelle, I can play piano, too, remember?" Anjali sat on the bench beside Noelle, found the E key, and began singing, "Jin gle bells, jin gle bells," while playing three consecutive notes.

Gabe came to stand behind Anjali. "Miss Noelle is preparing for an important concert, so let's go into the kitchen and give her some quiet time to practice, all right?"

Anjali continued to press the E key. "Mr. Gabe, do you know what note this is?"

121

His leaned over Noelle and Anjali. "I'm tone-deaf."

"That's okay. So is my Daddy, but everyone knows where Middle C is. Just find two black keys in the middle, and Middle C is the white key to the left," Anjali said.

Noelle pointed to Middle C, and Gabe reached around her and pressed the key three times. He sang, then gave a throaty laugh. "Thanks for giving me my first piano lesson."

"Any time," Noelle replied. "My rates are very competitive."

Anjali started playing again. "E is two notes up from Middle C. The piano is an alphabet." Anjali pressed three white keys in a row. "C, D, E."

"Thanks, Anjali. Let's go into the kitchen so that Miss Noelle can practice in private." Gabe scooped the little girl in his arms and carried her to the kitchen. "Can you help me pick out a flavor for a wedding cake that I've coerced your Mommy into baking for my cousin's wedding? Do you like chocolate or vanilla?" He turned, winked at Noelle, and mouthed, 'Have fun.'

Noelle practiced awkwardly at first, the pieces not making musical sense without the right hand melody. Her speed and accuracy suffered, and a slight heaviness weighed in her stomach with each wrong left hand note. Slowly, she tacked on new measures, drilling her left hand to play louder, then softer. Her senses heightened as she threw herself into the music, enjoying the intense, lush chords.

An hour and a half later, she was breathless. She stood and stretched, catlike. Her limbs felt lighter. Her practice session had gone well, the rapid arpeggios in her left hand never sounding better. Although she missed playing with two hands, she felt back on track, certain her right hand would heal quickly.

She wandered toward the kitchen, drawn by the enticing aromas of cinnamon and vanilla.

"All that music coming from one hand." Gabe made direct eye contact with Noelle and applauded. "You're amazing!"

"Bravo!" Mrs. Fernandez joined in the applause, along with Anjali. "I'd love to attend your concert, although I'll be too busy baking Christmas cookies."

Gabe grinned. "I'd love to attend, and I'm available because I'm not baking any Christmas cookies. I order them from Mrs. Fernandez," he said quickly.

Noelle tilted back her head, thinking she'd savor their encouraging responses to reflect on later. The day had gone much better than she'd anticipated, and although the burn stung, she'd pushed through the pain. Once the bandage came off, she'd double up her practice and be well-prepared for a triumphant comeback. She might be asked to book concerts all over the United States, perhaps even Europe.

This group of wonderful friends emboldened her with self-assurance, convinced her she'd made the right decision to accept Colin's offer to perform on the concert stage with him.

Her smile wavered when she surveyed the gay atmosphere of the Fernandez kitchen. Gabe and Anjali were carefully mixing cake batter, then measuring powdered sugar into a large stainless steel bowl. All the while, he answered Anjali's endless questions with relaxed nurturing and endless patience. Noelle could hardly tear her gaze from him. He was all male, yet he carried off complete absorption and enthusiasm in the art of cake baking.

Stepping into the kitchen, she paused, feeling a puzzling shyness. She was beginning to care for him more and more, and there was no point in denying her feelings.

"Miss Noelle, wanna try the vanilla butter cake Mommy's baking for Mr. Gabe's wedding? Mommy said we're taste-testing." Anjali toyed with a plateful of cake. "Butter is delicious!"

Gabe sliced a piece of cake, hot and crumbling from the oven. He offered the cake and a fork to Noelle. She accepted, appreciating every bite of the warm sweetness.

"I recommend a caramel butter cream filling if you choose the vanilla butter cake for the wedding," Mrs. Fernandez said.

"What kind of icing?" Gabe quizzed.

"Torched meringue."

Gabe regarded Noelle over a forkful of cake. "Try the pink champagne cake," he said. "Mrs. Fernandez recommended a rum filling and whipped cream frosting."

He watched Noelle closely as she enjoyed a bite of each. "Which do you prefer?"

Noelle tipped her head toward the pink cake and laid down her fork. "It's not my wedding, although I'm partial to anything pink, including pink champagne."

AFTERWARD Gabe insisted on treating Noelle to dinner at Snowing Rock country club.

"I'm not dressed properly," Noelle protested, although he assured her she looked stunning.

After hanging their outerwear in the front reception room of the country club, he escorted her to a table near a huge marble fireplace. Noelle glanced down at her black wool slacks, crisp white poplin shirt, and long, gray pleated cardigan. The thick gold carpeting, the sweeping expanse of glass looking out onto a snowy golf course prompted her to realize that she looked anything but stunning in the affluent surroundings.

Gabe, on the other hand, looked extraordinarily fine in navy wool pants and a pin-striped shirt, emphasizing his athletic shoulders. His tweedy gray wool scarf was slung loosely around his neck. His grin was so boyishly appealing when she'd agreed to accompany him to dinner, she couldn't help but smile.

He recommended thyme chicken with roasted potatoes and Mediterranean vegetables. "A specialty of the house," he declared.

An hour later, after finishing more food than she normally ate in a week, she leaned back in her heavy wooden chair and sighed. "As always, you've done too much for me."

"Are you depriving me of the joy I feel when I've made such a special woman happy?"

She grinned. His teasing question, along with his kindling hazel gaze, warmed her.

He reached for her left hand across the table. "I've waited fifteen years for this moment. I've wanted to take you to dinner at the country club ever since I was eighteen, dreaming I could someday afford this place." He hesitated. "Ever since the day you soundly scolded me and that bully at school. I remember your green eyes flashed like dueling swords when you shouted for us to stop fighting."

She laughed. "Apparently my flashing eyes didn't deter you from fighting that bully, anyway."

Gabe shrugged. "He left me no choice. He wanted to sell drugs to my cousin, Holly. Regardless of my attempts, Holly went through a hard time anyway, but she's furthered her education, she's industrious and adaptable, and I'm very proud of her."

"She sounds like a woman who's gone through a lot and persevered," Noelle said.

"Will you attend her wedding? I'd like you to meet her."

Noelle heard the guarded, hopeful note in Gabe's voice.

"We both know I'll be gone by then." Even as she spoke she debated. Although she was determined to return to Saint Augustine and perform, she wasn't as excited as she had been.

"You'll miss Mrs. Fernandez's delectable wedding cake," he said.

Noelle pushed the leftover roasted potatoes and eggplant around on her dinner plate. "Honestly, I'd love to attend, although to journey back to Snowing Rock from Saint Augustine ..." She sighed. "I suffer from motion sickness and it's a long bus ride."

"Then I'll arrange your flight from Saint Augustine to Fisher's Crossing." He caught her gaze. "Agree and tell me the matter's settled."

She smiled. "Okay. The matter's settled."

He went around the table, assisted her to her feet, and escorted her down the wall-papered hallway.

"And you can spend Christmas with me," he continued. "My cousin and her new husband will be honeymooning in the Bahamas and they're taking Devin along."

"I can't, really," Noelle protested. "Christmas is a special day and I'll want to spend the day with my aunt."

"You can both spend it with me." A roguish smile spread across Gabe's features. "You wouldn't want me to be alone on Christmas Day? What would I do with myself? I'll have no candles to make, no weddings to plan, no stunts to—"

She laughed. "Perhaps," she relented.

"And who's going to eat all that wedding cake?" He grinned mischievously and Noelle dissolved into a fit of laughter.

"You will! My waistline has probably doubled since I arrived."

Christmas in Snowing Rock with Gabe, she mused, wiping tears of mirth from her cheeks. A white, wonderful Christmas.

"Gabe Waters!" a lilting woman's voice came from the front reception room. "You've made yourself scarce since you've been back in town. You've only visited my place once."

Noelle swiveled to spot the ever-elegant Lucia Crandall strutting over. Lucia's hair was flawlessly arranged in her stylish pixie cut. She wore a tailored green silk suit, hugging her curvaceous, petite figure to perfection.

Gabe greeted Lucia, then turned to Noelle. "I'll get our coats."

Lucia's gaze traveled from Gabe to Noelle and her eyes narrowed. "I didn't expect to see you dining in a place like this." She swept out her arms, then studied Noelle's bandaged hand.

Noelle glimpsed herself in one of the ornate mirrors hanging on the country club's walls. She looked too pale, she decided, and her hair was unruly and uncombed. She shook back her blonde curls, feeling plain and unsophisticated beside the chic and well-groomed Lucia. Realizing that Lucia was regarding Noelle's bandaged hand expectantly, Noelle explained, "I burned my hand on candle wax after the candle class last night."

"Aren't you performing in a concert next month?" Lucia asked smoothly. "I know from experience that wax burns take weeks to heal, and you'll be left with a scar."

Gabe returned and assisted Noelle with her coat. "Ready to leave?" he asked.

Lucia placed a possessive hand on Gabe's wrist. "We're spending Thanksgiving together, remember?"

"As long as I'm back in town," he replied.

"No movie director will film over Thanksgiving weekend, so I'll be expecting you." Lucia swiveled to Noelle. "Don't forget the ladies club would enjoy background piano music for our Christmas luncheon." Lucia adjusted her fox fur coat around her shoulders. "We won't be able to pay you, though. Our club is in the red and I assume a famous pianist like you doesn't need the money, right?"

CHAPTER 11

Neither Gabe nor Noelle broke the charged silence on the drive to her aunt's stone cottage. Tiny snowflakes melted against the Land Rover's heated windshield, and purple clouds drifted slowly across a darkening sky.

Gabe pulled into the driveway and shut off the engine.

He glanced at Noelle's tight profile and sighed. For the first time since the bus accident, he didn't know how to begin their conversation.

She sat with her hands clasped together on her lap, staring straight ahead.

After a lengthy silence, she said, "You promised the burn would begin to heal within three days."

"I didn't promise, Noelle. I said a first-degree burn would heal in three to six days, and a second-degree burn would take two weeks. I'm not a doctor and —"

"And don't be a liar, either," she snapped.

He gazed at her reddened face. How could she charge him with lying? Didn't she know him at all? He'd built a successful career based on truthfulness and good character.

His tone deepened. "I spoke from my experience on movie sets. There have been horrific fires, and guys have been badly hurt. I know how long it took for them to heal."

"Lucia is a professional candle maker." Noelle's voice rose. "Lucia knows from experience."

"And I don't?" Heat flushed through his body, reliving the stunt he'd performed the day of the stunt accident, how he'd almost blacked out, the people who could've gotten hurt because he'd neglected to care for his diabetes properly.

"And when were you planning to tell me you'd be gone until Thanksgiving?" she asked.

Despite her infuriated tone, he couldn't help smiling to himself. She obviously cared for him or she wouldn't be so upset he was leaving.

"I got a call from Christopher Swidering, my agent, this morning, and I can't refuse the stunt because I'm under contract until the end of the year," he said. "I planned to tell you when we got back to the cottage. The director wants to film an action shot because the weather forecast in Wilmington calls for heavy rain, which is the weather they need for the shoot. Handling the logistics of a movie scene like this is mind-boggling, and there's little margin for error, and everyone has to be present. Can you change your bandages yourself?"

Her laughter had an edge. "I'm not an idiot, Gabe."

"I'll phone you when I arrive in Wilmington, all right? It's a short flight."

She reached for the passenger door handle. "I'll be busy at the candle shop or practicing piano. If I don't pick up, leave a message. Oh, and enjoy Thanksgiving dinner with Lucia."

He shot around the SUV and captured Noelle's arm as she stepped onto the driveway. He studied her high chin and flushed face for a beat, then explained evenly, "Months ago, I promised Lucia I'd take her to the country club for Thanksgiving because her husband had recently passed, and she didn't want to be alone for a holiday. She's an old friend."

Noelle stared at him with those flashing green eyes. "I couldn't care less about your relationship with Lucia."

"You've been glaring at me ever since we left the country club!"

She broke eye contact. "Of course your career comes first and my bandaged hand isn't a priority."

"I'll take Lucia to the club for Thanksgiving, then come to your place afterward." He rubbed his knuckles lightly across Noelle's smooth cheekbone and softened his voice. "Remember that sleigh ride I promised you?"

She bit her lip. "Of course I remember."

"We'll go on Thanksgiving night." He ran a hand through his hair. "In the meantime, say a prayer for me, all right? I'll be stunt driving a racecar on two wheels while accelerating. It's up to me to keep the car under control at a very high speed."

"Yes, I'll pray." She pulled at a wayward curl on her forehead. "Gabe, will you be safe?"

"No worries. I'm a pro, remember?"

"Yes, but still ..."

His conscience nagged at the way he'd navigated around her question. He'd offered factual information, although he'd skimmed over his response. Stunt driving almost always involved an element of danger.

His forefinger traced her trembling lips. "I like knowing you're a tad worried about me."

She fidgeted with her jacket. The creamy skin beneath her eyes was darkened by shadows.

"I'm very worried," she said.

"I also like knowing you're a tad jealous."

Her eyes widened. "I'm not the least bit jealous."

He swallowed a smile. "In any case, a send-off kiss will take away the sting of our disagreement. Agreed?"

She sighed, then nodded. His hands shifted to her back, molding her to his hard form. His lips touched hers, tentatively at first, growing bolder.

Drawing a long breath, she locked her arms around his neck.

Her tender kisses and light touch nearly swept away his self-control. They were in her aunt's driveway, the blast of a harsh winter wind piercing through the fabric of their clothes.

Although it was almost dusk, the neighbors were probably all watching.

His chest tightened. Damn the neighbors. Damn the contract.

As the kiss deepened, he considered canceling the gag in Wilmington altogether. The director could scramble and find someone else.

Although Gabe knew he wouldn't cancel, for he was a man whom people could count on.

An eternity later, he lifted his mouth from Noelle's, wanting to feel her sweet lips pressed against his one more time. Only she could take away his parents' neglect, his need to prove himself and overcome his disease, his resultant risky profession.

Wood-burning fireplaces and the smoky smell of seasoned saplings scented the air. Nightfall had crept in, the purple clouds had darkened, the tiny snowflakes had changed to a mist of silvery ice. Noelle quivered, and he kept his arm around her while he walked her to the cottage.

They settled together for a few moments on the living room couch. After he changed her bandages, he checked his watch.

"It's getting late," he said. "My flight leaves early for Wilmington."

She didn't meet his eyes. "I know."

"I'll miss you. You'll answer your phone when I call?"

She slanted a slight smile. "Unless I'm too busy practicing."

"Then I'll keep calling until you pick up the phone." He brushed a soft kiss on her upturned forehead, his mind racing with all the things he needed to pack for his upcoming trip as he strode out the door.

When he reached his Land Rover, he couldn't bring himself to start the engine and head out. Instead, he sat in the driver's seat, steepled his hands on the steering wheel, and gazed at the rustic stone cottage.

He didn't want to leave Noelle. She was in Snowing Rock for only a short time. He'd waited years for the chance to see her again because he knew he'd fallen in love with her, although he hadn't admitted that fact to himself until now.

Love. He shook his head in frustration. Hadn't he learned from an ill-starred marriage that love was an impractical, idealistic concept? How could he ever be truly loved and accepted when his own parents hadn't cared about him?

He scrubbed a hand over his face and sighed heavily. Besides, his occupation was too hazardous ... his disease too complicated.

The last few days he and Noelle had spent together, he'd sensed she was becoming more attracted to him. In several instances, she'd sought his reassurances and embraces of her own accord.

Just thinking of Colin, her contemptuous ex, infuriated Gabe. How could Colin dare to dictate what she should wear, how low she should bow...

Irritably, Gabe started the engine. He'd become preoccupied with an indescribably exquisite young woman who'd stolen his heart in a high school hallway.

He rubbed his whiskered chin. He needed a shave. Since Noelle had arrived in Snowing Rock, he'd neglected his work-outs. He decided to hit his home gym and string together a double routine and longer set before retiring for the evening, being sure to check his blood sugar levels beforehand. He hoped he wouldn't regret his decision in the morning. A stuntman couldn't perform a back flip over a speeding car with a limp.

CHAPTER 12

As Aunt Joy had predicted, the Wednesday before Thanksgiving was a quiet day at the candle shop with few customers. Noelle used the extra time to prepare for the shop's Black Friday sale, replenishing the shelves with tapered Christmas candles. Caroline had taken the day off to spend with Alan, promising to open the shop early on Friday morning.

An hour passed before Noelle greeted the first customer of the day, a red-haired woman with pin curls in her hair.

"Welcome to 'Scents of Joy'!" Noelle greeted with a wave. She was trying her best to be cheery, although she wasn't feeling it with Gabe gone.

The young woman acknowledged the greeting and raced through the shop, muttering and shaking her head as she picked up two cranberry scented votive candles. "I'm visiting my parents for Thanksgiving Day. Can you recommend an appropriate gift I can take?"

"Certainly." Noelle led the red-haired woman to a cornucopia featuring Wasabi Pear tapered candles and the woman quickly agreed with Noelle's recommendation. Noelle ran the woman's credit card transaction with no problem, then gift-wrapped the centerpiece.

"The pear scent is fresh and bright and the ideal candle to light after a heavy Thanksgiving dinner," Noelle explained.

After the customer departed, the remainder of the day dragged with few customers.

Before Noelle closed the shop at six o'clock, she unpacked tea light candles from a distributor. She frowned at some of the wicks because they were broken off and needed to be returned because the flame would never burn big or hot enough.

When she had finished and had tallied up the receipts, she glanced at her cell phone, anticipating her nightly conversation with Gabe. Although she hadn't seen him in two weeks, he'd phoned every evening. They'd talked for hours, about their work, about their pasts, about their high school and college years. He'd begun every conversation by asking for a detailed account of her burn wound and how it was healing.

But he wasn't in Snowing Rock, and his lifestyle meant that he couldn't be depended on. Obviously, she wasn't his main concern.

She'd continued with the care he'd initiated, washing her hands and cleansing the wound thoroughly, applying antibiotic cream, and wrapping the wound in a clean bandage. There'd been no signs of infection, and within a week the dead, burned skin had peeled off and new red skin had healed to a light pink.

When she'd inquired about Gabe's work, he'd dismissed the action film as a 'typical racing car flick.' When she'd pressed for details, knowing the film would most likely become another box office hit, he'd described action shots involving his jump from a twenty-foot cliff, or throwing his racecar into a skid, or flipping the racecar over while he drove.

She'd hold her breath, sometimes wishing she hadn't asked, telling him she felt sure that her hair was turning prematurely gray and she was developing a new wrinkle with every death-defying feat he'd described.

He'd laughed softly. "Airbags help," he'd finished.

Her piano practice had lessened as a result of their lengthy conversations, although she'd been able to squeeze in three hours every evening.

Gabe cared about her, he obviously desired her. And although she had little faith in deciphering her own emotions, she wouldn't deny her growing feelings for him, despite her fears of becoming vulnerable. That focused, powerful stuntman left no doubt that he wanted to be with her.

Fortunately, her aunt's piano had been fixed by the competent piano technician from Fisher's Crossing. The technician had replaced the damper pedal rod, fastened the pins on the upper and lower levers of the piano, and tuned the piano.

Although Gabe wasn't expected to return to Snowing Rock until Thanksgiving morning, Noelle occasionally caught herself looking up from the cash register when a customer walked in, half-expecting him to stride in and place another order for vanilla-scented beeswax candles. She could just hear him saying, 'To repay my kindness in adding to your sales, all I want is a sugar cookie in return.'

THE FOLLOWING AFTERNOON, Noelle went to the rehab center to enjoy Thanksgiving dinner with Aunt Joy. After saying grace, she and her aunt were seated at a long, rectangular table along with several other senior citizens convalescing from a range of injuries.

Long after Noelle had eaten more than her share of thyme-filled turkey, fluffy sweet potatoes topped with marshmallows, and a mountain of mashed potatoes drowning in boiled gravy, she sat back, hoping she'd still be able to fit into her black recital gown.

As the meal came to a close, Noelle lightly rapped her fingers along the tablecloth, practicing the first measure of Chopin.

Her aunt giggled affection beneath a wide-brimmed straw hat and evened out her long, lime-green skirt so that it stretched to her ankles.

"I'm so happy you came to Snowing Rock," she said.

Noelle smiled in agreement. "After holidays alone in Saint Augustine, it's good to celebrate with family."

"Holidays are about spending time with the people who matter most in your life, dear." Aunt Joy patted Noelle's arm, then dove into a creamy slice of pumpkin pie topped with whipped cream. "Your hand healed with little scarring," she observed.

"And I've practiced all week with two hands!" Noelle yanked the sleeves up on her black cashmere sweater and waved both hands in the air. "Gabe was right!"

"And where is your Gabe?" Aunt Joy prompted.

"He's not my Gabe," Noelle said.

Her aunt managed a wan smile. "Aren't things between you going well?"

"I'm seeing him tonight, after he's taken Lucia Crandall to dinner at the country club."

Aunt Joy's fork froze in mid-bite. "He was welcome to dine with us at the rehab center."

Noelle rubbed the back of her neck. "He couldn't. He'd promised Lucia."

Although Noelle attempted to exude calmness, she felt her muscles tighten. Gabe's friendship with Lucia and his Thanksgiving promise were reasons enough why Noelle needed to return to Saint Augustine and succeed.

Noelle didn't respond to her aunt's upraised, penciled-in brow. Instead, she glanced at her cell phone. There'd been no messages from him since they'd spoken last evening. Still, if his flight had been delayed, he'd have contacted her.

"You always steer the conversation to me, Aunt Joy," Noelle said. "I'm glad you'll be back at the candle shop before I leave on December thirteenth. Although Caroline is knowledgeable, I want to learn the candle business from you, the woman who started it all."

"I'd love to see your performance in Saint Augustine. However, between running the shop and recovering from my hip injury—"

"And I'd love for you to attend," Noelle parroted, checking her aunt's explanation in mid-sentence. "Nonetheless, I completely understand. And, Colin emailed me last night. Ticket sales are brisk and the concert's slated to be broadcast on an FM classical radio station, so

I'll give you the station's info and you can listen to the performance live."

Silently, Noelle cringed at the thought that her performance would be recorded. If she had a memory slip, would her audience judge her again?

She leaned back in her chair and took an easy breath. She could do this. She was skilled, and Gabe's nightly encouragements had deepened her resolve.

Her cell phone pinged, and she viewed Gabe's text message: 'Arrived safely. Rushed home for a shower, now at the country club for the quickest Thanksgiving dinner Lucia will ever eat. See you at 5. Ready for a sleigh ride?' He'd inserted a heart emoji.

'Yes,' she texted back. She'd make good on her promise to go to the O'Donnell farm with him.

A few minutes later, she bid her aunt farewell with a fierce hug.

The sun was setting as Noelle headed toward the cottage. While she drove, she admired snow-capped pine trees, the branches shimmering in the last wanes of sunlight. A fat snowman with a carrot nose stood on a street corner, most likely made by happy, squealing children.

She steered into the driveway, surprised to see Gabe's familiar black Land Rover pull in behind her. Simultaneously, they both shut off their engines. He vaulted from his vehicle and drew her into his arms before she'd taken two steps.

She stiffened.

"I missed you." He dropped his hands, stepped back, and examined her right hand. "Only a slight scar left from the burn."

"And my Chopin is much better. I've refined my phrasing and articulation."

"I'm proud of you, Noelle," he said.

"You can enjoy my concert along with the entire listening audience on the FM radio station." She shook the curls from her face and asked the question that had nagged at her all afternoon. "How was Thanksgiving dinner with Lucia?"

Gabe scowled, then shrugged dismissively. "Quick. How was Thanksgiving dinner with your aunt?"

"Very enjoyable. I admire Aunt Joy's business sense more each day. My mother used to complain that Aunt Joy was a non-conformist, although I've come to realize that's a good trait."

"She sounds remarkable, like her niece." Gabe slipped his arm around her shoulders and guided her to his SUV, opening the passenger door for her. "Are you ready for the sleigh ride?"

She nodded. That morning, she'd dressed ahead for the arctic-like night air, wearing a cashmere sweater and woolen hat, leggings, thick coat, and leather boots.

When they'd settled into Gabe's Land Rover, she asked, "How did filming go in Wilmington?"

"The rain was nonstop and made the stunts more difficult." Gabe enhanced his statement with a theatrical groan. "Fortunately, they called a wrap, unless there's a moment in the film the director believes needs to be improved with a reshoot. Consequently, I can attend your piano performance in Saint Augustine, so I won't need to listen to it on the radio."

"You might be bored ... you're a stunt racecar driver ... don't you prefer action?"

"I promise I won't embarrass you and fall asleep during the performance. I'll be the person in the audience clapping the loudest."

Cautiously, she ventured, "Colin said he'd give me a complimentary ticket."

"How generous of him." Gabe scoffed, then softened his tone. "Tell him I want a front row center seat."

Her old fears emerged. Could she trust Gabe to keep his promise and attend her concert? Could she take him at his word?

What if she had a memory lapse? Would he see her as a failure? Anything could go wrong during a live performance. Just thinking about it made her feel nauseated and sick to her stomach.

No, she told herself adamantly. She'd conquered her silent terror. Besides, this performance wasn't about her. She was giving something back to her audience, her gift of music.

As they drove in silence, passing a crisp, winter-white landscape, she asked, "Do you know the route to the O'Donnell farm?"

He smiled. "Like the back of my hand."

As they approached the left turn onto a private drive, Noelle leaned forward. "Why is there a high security fence around the entire property?"

"To keep out the paparazzi," Gabe explained vaguely.

She crossed her arms and focused on the high iron fence. "Do celebrities come to the

O'Donnell farm to take sleigh rides and buy Christmas trees?"

He didn't answer. Instead, he idled the SUV and pressed a code at the entrance. The front gate swung to the side, and they followed a long driveway past acres of fir trees, the branches heavy with snow. They didn't stop, as she'd expected, at a wood-framed caretaker's cottage, aglow with flickering lights within, nor at an imposing red barn farther down the road. The distance widened and a magnificent, tri-level mansion loomed ahead.

Gabe drove his Land Rover to the entrance. He turned off the engine, got out and came around to open the passenger door for her.

She stepped out. Large flakes were beginning to fall and the air seemed quiet, her footsteps muffled.

"Why are we stopping here?" She tilted her head, surveying the main level wood deck wrapping around the impressive home. "Who lives—?"

"I do, Noelle. Do you approve of my cabin in the woods?"

CHAPTER 13

N oelle gasped and became still for a moment. "How big is this ... cabin ... er ... mansion?" she asked in a loud voice.

Gabe grinned as she stared in wide-eyed bewilderment at him. "About ten thousand square feet," he said.

"Are you the O'Donnell's caretaker?"

He laughed and shook his head. "I'm the owner. I bought the home and surrounding acreage a few years ago and fixed everything up. Actually, my cousin, Holly, oversaw the remodel and interior design. Want to see the inside?"

"Yes, of course."

He tucked her hand in the crook of his arm and led her to the covered front porch. They admired stunning mountain views before entering the spacious foyer.

"The house is on three levels," Gabe nodded toward the opulent central staircase and elevator and flicked on a low, overhead light. "On the left is the formal living room. I haven't found the proper furniture, so it's empty except for a couch and chair."

She removed her coat and red wool hat, shaking her blonde curls free. He took their outerwear and hung their coats in the entry closet.

They walked to the living room and she glided toward the floor to ceiling windows. Gazing outside, she said, "A piano would go perfectly between these windows and the stone fireplace. And I can see the entire town of Snowing Rock." She whirled to face him. "You can arrange Christmas candles on the fireplace mantel. The shop just got in a new fragrance — chutney and cranberry."

Moonlight glinted through the glass, enhancing her soft skin to a rose-colored hue, giving her an ethereal appearance.

He paused, admiring her. "I don't need candles. You're so lovely, you light up the entire room."

She began walking toward him with that graceful elegance he'd always marveled at. "Your home is splendid, Gabe," she finished softly.

"Not as splendid as you." He closed the distance and slid his arm around her. "And something else of great importance is lacking in my home besides a piano."

"What's that?" she asked.

Noelle Wentworth, he thought to himself.

Aloud, he replied, "A sprig of mistletoe hanging in the doorway."

She leaned against the wall. "Gabe, it's not Christmas yet."

He braced his hands on the wall above her shoulders. "Do you remember Snowing Rock High's Christmas dance fifteen years ago?"

"Yes, my aunt and I discussed that dance recently."

"You wore a red sequined dress. You looked irresistible."

"I couldn't wait to leave," she said.

"And I also remember a mistletoe in the doorway." Briefly, his lips descended on hers. "I wanted to claim you for a dance and kiss you under the mistletoe. I turned to get some tortilla chips and you were gone."

Her cheeks pinkened. "I remember running through that doorway as fast as I could."

"Next time there's mistletoe, I won't turn around. And if you run, I'll catch you."

He bent his head to kiss her again, then checked himself. She seemed distant.

He sighed. Although he felt a sense of pride to show her his home, the home he'd worked so hard and so long for, he also felt the need to take things slowly.

"There's a wood-paneled library with a fireplace beyond, a guest bedroom, and sitting areas on this level," he said. "I'll show you the upper level first, all right?"

When they reached the top of the staircase, he guided her to the chef's kitchen containing a large breakfast nook, a family room anchored by a large fireplace, and the master suite with another fireplace adding romance to the decor. He led her out to the private balcony that held a hot tub, and they stared at the expansive snow-capped peaks, the moonlit shadows dancing in the cobblestone courtyard below.

He stood behind her with his chin resting on her hair. Ever so slightly, she leaned back against him. He stirred at the intense feeling of her body pressed to his, and his hand fell to her waist and pulled her closer.

For a moment, he debated about asking her to marry him right where they stood. They could plan a Christmas wedding within the next few weeks, send invitations, spend their honeymoon anywhere in the world. He'd explain his diabetes, a topic he'd avoided, hoping she wouldn't view him as a weakling and lose respect for him. He wanted her to see him as strong and dependable.

His mind explored wedding arrangements before he reluctantly forced the idea aside.

Noelle needed to concentrate on her upcoming performance. Despite her fearlessness, he assumed she still harbored insecurities and stage fright. Afterward, she'd be able to concentrate on rebuilding her self-esteem and he, in turn, would offer safety and security.

Since he couldn't ask her to marry him yet, he murmured into her fragrant hair the only other thought that was important to him.

"Noelle Wentworth, I love you. I've always loved you."

He felt the poignant effect of his words because she stiffened. With a graceful twirl in his arms, she lifted her gorgeous face to his.

"I'm slowly learning to trust again," she said quietly. "Give me time."

He wrapped his arms around her and bent his head, his lips moving over hers. She stood on her toes, hesitantly kissing him back. When he lifted his lips, he murmured, "I'm a patient man and I'll wait for you. Always remember you can trust me." Reluctantly, he released his grip and gazed into her jade-green eyes.

"I trust you more than I've trusted anyone in a long time," she said.

Her response made his throat tighten.

He held her hand as they rode to the lower level in his private elevator. The level boasted a work-out room with state of the art exercise equipment, a family room with fireplace, and a large projection theater room.

"Isn't tonight the opening for your film, 'Force of Thunder Two'?" she asked.

"I'm not comfortable watching my films," he replied. "I tried once, with Devin, and ended up leaving the room after ten minutes because I scrutinized every mistake."

They rode the elevator to the upper level and strolled to the kitchen.

"I bought you a gift while I was in Wilmington." He indicated a small box wrapped with red foil paper and tied with a gold bow lying on the table. "It was special ordered."

She arched her delicate brows questioningly at the small package. "I'm assuming this isn't a bouquet of flowers," she said. Carefully, she unwrapped the gift and spread the printed words on the table.

"I bought you a tattoo," he said. "You mentioned you'd always wanted one. Unlike mine, yours isn't permanent and should last only a week or two." He read the words aloud, "'Running away from your problems is a race you'll never win.'" A snowy mountain against a blue-gray sky loomed in the background.

An incredulous beam broke across her face. "This tattoo is the same as yours."

"Yes, we'll match." He studied her, his thoughts drifting to the day when he could ask her to be his wife. Her sweetness warmed his heart.

He cleared his throat. "You could've run far away from the concert stage, you could've hidden—"

"I did," she said.

"You mustered up the courage to face your problem head-on. Not many people have that kind of determination."

She raked her fingers through her hair. "In case you haven't noticed, I'm not the sort of person who wears tattoos, despite what I might've said in a moment of weakness."

"Yours is a temporary henna tattoo." He rolled up the shirtsleeves of his navy blue sweater, exposing his right forearm with the same words tattooed in permanent ink.

She took a quick breath and bit her bottom lip. "My tattoo will come off before my concert, right? My gown is sleeveless and Colin would be furious."

"And Colin can answer to me from now on. Here, take a seat." Gabe pulled out a kitchen stool and shifted his gaze to her pasted-on half-smile. "Noelle Wentworth, you're not nervous, are you?"

"Not a bit," she said, eyeing the doorway before settling on the stool.

He rolled up the right sleeve of her black cashmere sweater. She closed her eyes and breathed in.

"No needles, I promise, and this will take less than a minute." He wet a sponge from the sink and brought back a pair of scissors to the table. He felt Noelle's entire right side clench as he wet and applied the tattoo with firm and gentle pressure, then peeled off the backing.

"You're done?" she asked.

"In less than a minute."

She examined her tattooed forearm. "'Running away from your problems is a race you'll never win.'" She grinned. "Somehow, having a tattoo makes me feel giddy and reckless!" She rolled down her sleeve and sighed. "I hope I can show it off."

"Saint Augustine doesn't have Snowing Rock's winter weather," Gabe replied. "On the other hand, every time you look at your tattoo, think of me. I'll do the same."

"You're good to me, Gabe." Her eyes welled with tears. He snuggled her against his chest, her words muffling against his heart.

He offered her a white handkerchief from his pocket. "If you cry whenever I give you a gift, be prepared to have dozens of handkerchiefs with you at all times, because I intend to shower you with endless presents."

She drew back and dabbed at her eyes. Her lips twitched. "You mean showering me with endless tattoos?"

"As many as you want."

The night sky was dotted with stars by the time Gabe guided her to the front foyer and retrieved their coats. "Tomorrow's an early morning for you at the candle shop. I'll text Stan, my caretaker, to harness the draft horses for our sleigh ride."

"Don't tell me you have a caretaker?"

"I can't manage this entire property by myself. We passed his cottage on the way in. He lives there with his wife, Elise, who cleans my house and sometimes leaves a meal for me. She's an excellent cook, and although I've reserved Snowing Rock Country Club to cater Holly's wedding, Elise will be there to supervise. I'll also show you the renovated barn for the reception. I could use some guidance because I can't begin to comprehend—"

"Gabe, sounds like every detail has been planned to perfection, including the candles."

"There's always details that I miss."

And the main detail that was missing was his beautiful Noelle standing by his side. How could his house ever feel like a home without her?

161

CHAPTER 14

A unt Joy had been right about Black Friday sales, Noelle reflected, looking back on how busy the shop had been on the Friday after Thanksgiving. Her aunt had also predicted how hectic the following days would become, stuffed with customers and roaring with activity. It didn't matter. Noelle felt comfortable in her surroundings, and happy working at the shop.

Two weeks had spun by in a marvelous blur. Noelle had purchased her dress for Holly's wedding ahead of time in one of the upscale boutiques in town. The red sequined tea-length gown featured sheer sleeves and a pleated, taffeta skirt. The fitted, deep v-neckline bodice was delicately enhanced with gold embellishments. She'd described the dress to Gabe, and he'd kissed her, tenderly and deeply. With a tigerish gleam, he'd remarked that he looked forward to Holly's wedding so that he could see Noelle dressed like an exquisite goddess, and he planned to kiss her under the mistletoe he'd purposely hang in the doorway of his home.

Noelle smiled. The future looked bright, almost too good to be true.

She spent her daylight hours at the candle shop while Gabe donated endless amounts of energy to his outreach center. Evenings, she and Gabe were inseparable. They alternated between bringing dinner and dining with either Aunt Joy or the Fernandez family on weeknights, and enjoying a sumptuous meal at the country club on weekends. Afterward, Noelle would practice piano at her aunt's cottage, taking a few moments between pieces to get up and stretch. Gabe sat in the kitchen, humming quietly and out of tune, while learning new stunt skills and networking with other stuntmen online.

Noelle had recommended fun, upbeat recorded music for his outreach center's upcoming Christmas musical. When they visited the center, she watched him admiringly while he interacted with the teens, especially those teens who were disadvantaged and at high-risk. Gabe encouraged their self-confidence, advising them to choose their friends wisely while clarifying his personal values. They were his fans, and thus, listened to him. In turn, he was always generous, attentive, and supportive.

He was also the most attractive man Noelle had ever met. More and more, she felt appreciated and cared for, protected and loved.

The day before Noelle departed for Saint Augustine, Aunt Joy returned to the candle shop. Just before the shop closed, Noelle knelt in the front window and arranged a lighted holiday display.

Gabe strode in, turned automatically to the front window, and bent to plant a kiss on Noelle's lips. "You and I are booked roundtrip from Fisher's Crossing to Saint Augustine tomorrow," he said, straightening.

Noelle continued to arrange white pillar candles in a glass container, wrapping greenery around the base. "I bought a round-trip bus ticket, remember?" she absently corrected him.

He held out a pair of airline tickets. "You're performing the most important performance of your career, and you don't need the extra worry of motion sickness. The plane ride will shorten your travel to Saint Augustine and I'll be with you."

She came to her feet and examined the tickets.

"Our return tickets are open-ended with a flexible date." He grinned broadly. "Although I may return earlier, whereas you may need a few extra days in Saint Augustine to sign autographs and book concerts and arrange your permanent move to Snowing Rock."

"Did I say I was moving here permanently?" she laughed.

He pressed his lips on hers for a leisurely kiss. "If you require extra persuading ..."

"Your beeswax candles have arrived, Mr. Waters! Now we're just waiting for the Candleglow and Mistletoe candles," Caroline and Aunt Joy shouted at the same time as they emerged from the back storage room. Caroline's arms were laden with boxes while Aunt Joy stopped to price a soy candle.

Caroline placed the boxes on the counter near the cash register, then joined Gabe and Noelle in the front display window. Slowly, Caroline flicked a skinny blue braid from her face and tapped Gabe's arm. "Mr. Waters, after supplying you with enough candles to light the entire town of Snowing Rock, we all expect invitations to your cousin's wedding."

"Holly said she mailed out the invitations and you're all invited," Gabe answered.

Apparently not one to be pacified so quickly, Caroline turned another tack. "Alan and I have never visited Hawaii. Did you purchase any extra airline tickets to warm, tropical places?"

Gabe's shoulders shook with noiseless laughter as he retrieved Noelle's coat and slipped it around her. "Sorry. I'm only offering Saint Augustine tickets today, and they're both claimed and booked."

And this, Noelle thought with a beam, was why she loved Snowing Rock. Because of the supportive friends and family and splendid man she could rely on. Completely contented, she leaned against Gabe's arm as he opened the door for her, took her hand in his, and escorted her out of the shop. Scenic Snowing Rock reminded her of a Swiss mountain village, laced with aromas from hot chocolate and homemade gingerbread stands, a layer of pure white snow on the sidewalks. Miles of sparkling Christmas lights decorated timbered roofs and stone fences.

Christmas was definitely in the fresh mountain air.

As she and Gabe strolled slowly hand in hand, her feet dragged. She really wasn't excited about the prospect of leaving this special town where she now felt very much at home.

The following day passed quickly as Noelle packed her luggage and carry-on for her trip.

Despite his assurances, the henna tattoo Gabe had applied on Thanksgiving Day hadn't disappeared, despite endless scrubbing and applying oil on the tattoo.

She shrugged. No matter. Colin could fume all he wanted. Gabe would be with her, supporting and cheering, beginning with their plane ride to Saint Augustine.

EXCEPT THAT GABE wasn't able to accompany her on the plane.

Three hours before their scheduled departure, he'd phoned and explained that the director hadn't approved one of the film's action scenes, pouring rain was predicted in Wilmington, and Gabe had been requested to return for one last stunt before the shoot was considered a wrap and ready to go into post-production.

Noelle lowered her head and covered her face with her hands. "Can't your agent just call the director and tell him you have other plans?"

"I could never renege on this gag. The entire film would be delayed. They need me."

Noelle's stomach had clenched as he continued to expound on the details.

'What about me? I need you, too,' she'd wanted to say, although she said nothing, silently berating herself for wanting him near and relying on him, while knowing millions of dollars were at stake when producing a box-office hit.

"The scene will take less than a half day to film. I'll fly from Wilmington directly to Saint Augustine, all right?" Gabe was saying. He gave her his agent, Chris Swidering's, cell phone number in case she needed to reach Gabe while he was working.

A heavy sigh accompanied her words. "I'll arrange for the box office to hold your ticket."

"I'll be there. When you step onto the stage, look for me in the center of the first row. I'll be the guy who can't keep his eyes off you."

"And the guy who'll clap the loudest," she added with false cheer.

Because he was a man of his word. Wasn't he?

CHAPTER 15

In her dressing room at the Forum Theater, Noelle subjected herself to a full-length mirror scrutiny while she zipped up her black gown and adjusted a thin, rhinestone belt at her waist. Despite her concern that she'd gained weight, the gown still fit, clinging to her slender curves. She scrutinized the henna tattoo, boldly emblazoned on her right forearm.

'Every time you look at your tattoo, think of me. I'll do the same,' Gabe had said.

His words filled her with confidence, and she straightened her posture. Besides, there was no point in worrying about any shocked reactions because of an innocent henna tattoo.

Sitting at her dressing table, she drew her blonde curls severely up and back, threading a red velvet ribbon through her hair to contrast with the color of her black gown. Gabe had said he liked her hair that way because the style accentuated her high cheekbones.

She applied stage make-up with an exaggerated hand, knowing that otherwise her complexion would appear washed out under harsh onstage lights. Cream-colored foundation was followed by black mascara, muted red lipstick, and a fine dusting of light powder on her face.

Her dressing room was filled with the light, sweet scent of dozens of baby-pink rose bouquets, along with a hand-written card, all from Gabe. A bottle of rosé sparkling pink champagne sat chilling in a tall silver urn.

'We'll celebrate your success together after your performance, so look for me in the front row, all right?' the card read.

Then where was he? She'd checked her cell phone non-stop for the past hour, and had even phoned his agent and left a message.

She sank stiffly into a chair and briefly closed her eyes, reflecting on the previous afternoon's events. Colin had demanded a methodical run-through of their entire performance during dress rehearsal. Two seven foot grand pianos had been tuned and retuned, and acoustics checked. Several difficult sections had required practice at slower tempos with a metronome ticking steadily in the background.

After three hours of rehearsing, Colin had finally taken his hands off the piano keys and stretched his arms out wide. He'd swaggered over to Noelle's piano and surveyed her with a satisfied expression. "That went well."

"Your father will be pleased," she said.

Colin had slowly shaken his head. "My father passed last year, soon after you and I were divorced."

"I'm sorry, I didn't know," Noelle replied. "I'm sure you miss him."

"I think of him every time I play piano." Colin had replied.

Noelle had wiped the sweat from her hairline and raised her face to a welcome blast of air-conditioning. Saint Augustine's sub-tropical climate at Christmas was typical beach weather, and she'd chuckled at the garland-wrapped palm trees outside the terminal entrance when she'd landed at the airport.

"As soon as our gig is completed, I'm returning to Snowing Rock," she'd said to Colin.

Gig, not gag, she'd smiled to herself, thinking of Gabe.

"How can you put up with those mountain hillbillies sitting in their rocking chairs, spending their days watching the snow fall?" Colin had smirked.

"You couldn't be more wrong," she'd said.

Colin had shrugged, his gaze brightening. "Our ticket sales have been phenomenal. After the concert, you'll be paid a flat fee of five thousand dollars per our agreement. I knew my advertising would pay off—the estranged husband and wife duo teaming up for a Christmas reunion."

"You didn't pay for advertising, the Forum Theater did," she'd contradicted. "And the revenue from a full house will be well over sixty thousand dollars."

"You're calculating gross ticket sales," Colin had said. "You've never had my shrewd business sense. I have promoters to pay, the venue ..." he'd sighed dramatically.

"You were paid a flat rate of forty thousand dollars," she'd said. "I checked. And I deserve half. Twenty thousand dollars."

"You agreed to five thousand and — "

"I changed my mind. Our agreement was verbal. We didn't shake hands, nor was there a witness."

Colin had cracked his knuckles. She'd forgotten how much she'd disliked that.

"Be grateful I've given you a second chance to redeem your career," he'd said.

"And be grateful I'm one half of your success. Enjoy this concert, because it'll be the last time we'll be performing together."

Her thoughts snapped to the present by an insistent rap on her dressing room door, followed by an usher reminding Noelle that curtain time was in five minutes.

She stood and placed Gabe's card on her dressing table.

Now was the moment she'd been anticipating for months, the night of her successful return to the concert stage. She checked her appearance in the mirror, smoothing her gown with clammy hands. Sure, she was nervous and struggled with stage fright, and she'd learned to channel her nervous adrenaline into a dynamic performance. This performance would be no exception. She paused and whispered a silent prayer, thanking God for her natural abilities and talent.

Before she left the dressing room, she checked her cell phone once more, hoping Gabe had sent a text message. Perhaps he'd lost cell phone service because he was on a plane. Perhaps he'd gone directly to the Forum Theater as soon as he'd landed and hadn't had time to call.

The air-conditioning made her shiver. Perhaps he'd gotten hurt during the stunt?

No, she decided wretchedly. His agent would've contacted her.

She took a determined breath, reminding herself that she was a professional and expected on stage, no matter her personal life. With her head held high, she marched into the hallway and turned a glittering, artificial smile on Colin. Despite the fact that Colin employed a professional tailor, the sleeves and pants of his white tuxedo were too short.

Colin's gaze fastened on her right forearm. He loosened his collar. His face reddened. "What the hell is that?"

"It's a—"

He jerked his arm out dismissively to silence her. "I know what it is." He snapped his fingers and an usher appeared. "Does anyone have a sweater to put over this woman's shoulders?"

Noelle stood tall. "I won't cover myself. If you don't like the tattoo, then perform this two-piano concert by yourself."

"Thirty seconds," the usher advised.

Colin scowled.

"And we never finished our conversation from last evening. I want my fair share. Twenty thousand dollars," Noelle said.

"I've already spent the money on a new—" His voice rose to a falsetto.

"If you don't agree, then go on stage and explain to the audience."

The usher wrung her hands. "Ten seconds."

"Shut up!" Colin snapped to the usher.

"Agreed?" Noelle held out her hand for Colin to shake. She glanced at the usher. "You're our witness if he reneges."

"Yes, I agree!" Colin roughly grabbed Noelle's hand and shook. They walked onstage to resounding opening applause, dropped hands, and bowed deeply to the audience.

Noelle's gaze milled the crowd, searching for a handsome, tall man sitting in the front center seat. The gleam in his gaze when they made eye contact would convey his affection and support.

Except his seat was conspicuously empty.

Terrifyingly close to tears, she tried to convince herself this aching letdown was because she'd finally summoned up the courage to trust someone again. However, the desolate ache in her gut sprang from more than that. She wanted him to share in her important night.

As she walked to the grand piano and gazed at the black and white keys, a memory flooded her thoughts.

'Mr. Gabe, do you know what note this is?' Anjali had asked Gabe when he'd joined them at the Fernandez's piano.

His hard chest had pressed against Noelle's back as he'd joked, 'I'm tone-deaf.'

How, with them being so different, could she ever think they could make a life together, that she could trust and depend on him?

Silently, Noelle shook her head. She couldn't think about him now. She was a seasoned performer who was expected to remain focused.

With precise movements, she seated herself on the cushioned artist's bench and placed the music stand down, indicating her music was memorized. She poised her hands above the keys and made eye contact with Colin on the other side of the stage.

'Ready?' He mouthed.

She nodded curtly. Determined to enjoy this performance, she broke into the fast, opening bars of the Chopin etude, using the damper pedal sparingly. The acoustics in the concert hall absorbed the piano sound, and she relied on hand memory to take over the keys.

AN HOUR AND A HALF LATER, the concert was over.

Noelle had panicked for a split second during the Brahms, when her hand had slipped off the black keys when she'd played rapid octaves. The slip hadn't gone unnoticed by Colin, who'd glowered at her from his piano. Briefly paralyzed by fear of a memory lapse, she'd quickly extricated herself from her tight spot by relaxing and breathing in, then centering her attention on the music.

After she and Colin had performed the final notes of the Rachmaninoff finale, they both waited in silence until the music died away. Only then did they lift their fingers from the keys.

Noelle placed her hands in her lap and exhaled. Sweat poured down her back at the physical and emotional exertion involved in performing a vast amount of difficult repertoire.

Judging from the audience's shouts of 'bravo!', the concert had been a success, and she felt an emotional connection to her receptive and enthusiastic listeners. Her audience had forgiven her. In fact, they were embracing her.

Clapping grew faster and faster. She stood and turned, scanning the crowd for Gabe.

His seat was unfilled, and she swallowed hard. She'd performed the most brilliant concert of her career, and he hadn't been there. After countless hours humming the opening bars of Chopin while she'd practiced, he'd chosen his stunt job over her.

With one hand at her side, the other placed on the piano, she bowed to a standing ovation. Colin did likewise. They joined hands in the center of the stage and bowed deeply. As they'd rehearsed innumerable times, they straightened, smiled at the audience, and walked off the stage.

After another entrance and exit to great, gratifying applause, Noelle raced to her dressing room, shut the door, and snatched up her cell phone. Surely Gabe had called or texted. Her hands shook as she scanned the messages, consisting of only a missed phone call from Aunt Joy, as well as two congratulatory text messages, one from Mrs. Fernandez, the other from Caroline.

In desperation, she dialed his agent's cell phone again.

Christopher Swidering answered on the first ring. He stated rather vaguely that, yes, Gabe had finished the film shoot later than planned and been detained for several hours afterward before boarding a plane for New York City. Christopher, suddenly pleading busyness, had apologized for not returning her earlier call and hastily broke the connection.

Noelle sank into her dressing room chair. Gabe hadn't flown to Saint Augustine, he'd flown to New York City.

An usher knocked, delivering the news that several fans waited in the hallway for autographs. Also, the usher continued, Mr. Rudovich wanted a word with Noelle.

Pleading exhaustion, Noelle instructed the usher to apologize to her fans, close her dressing room door, and tell Mr. Rudovich to mail her check.

Noelle lowered her chin to her chest, anger and disappointment tramping dizzily through her mind. Somehow, she needed to stand, collect herself, and walk out of the Forum Theater.

She couldn't, her mind screamed. She needed to be alone.

She stepped to the full-length mirror and studied the tattoo.

'Running away from your problems is a race you'll never win.'

'Words to live by,' Gabe had said.

Perhaps she should call him. Anxiously, she wiped her palms along the folds of her black gown and picked up her cell phone. But what would she say if he answered?

Noelle trooped out of the Forum Theater, leaving Gabe's numerous rose bouquets, his card declaring that they'd celebrate together, and his bottle of pink champagne behind. She seated herself in the back of the taxi she'd called earlier, giving the driver her high-rise apartment address. Thankfully, the theater had cleared quickly and the sidewalks were empty. Colin was most likely celebrating in a fancy nightclub with his critic friends.

The taxi sped through muggy Saint Augustine streets, past a Santa Claus electronic display brilliantly flashing red 'ho, ho, ho' across a giant screen. Animated Christmas displays and wax myrtle trees were illuminated with white lights.

She sagged against the worn taxi seat and closed her eyes, her heart thudding dully in her chest. She'd imagined a fun-filled, snowy Christmas with Gabe. Now she'd be celebrating alone in Saint Augustine. A big city, just like New York City.

Her eyes snapped open and she jolted upright, recalling Lucia's conversation with Caroline on Noelle's first day at the candle shop.

'Did I mention I'm opening a second shop in New York City?' Lucia had asked.

New York City. Gabe was flying to New York City.

No, it couldn't be. Lucia and Gabe were just old friends.

Nonetheless, tears filled Noelle's eyes and she blinked them away. Her chest felt heavy. Loneliness and disbelief hurtled through her mind. Once again, she'd been a gullible, insecure fool.

She retrieved her cell phone from her purse to return Aunt Joy's phone message. Despite the late hour, concert offers were flooding Noelle's email inbox and optimism burst like a silvery ray of hope in the midst of a thunderstorm.

Her chin lifted. The heaviness in her chest lightened.

She'd sought esteem and recognition for all her hard work and she'd achieved her goal. She'd succeeded in reaching her dreams, hadn't she?

Then why was she crying?

CHAPTER 16

O ver the next few days, Noelle immersed herself in responding to concert venues across the country. With brave determination, she purposely kept herself too busy to think about Gabe. She'd answered text messages from both Mrs. Fernandez and Caroline with the same untruthful response. 'Thanks for your support. Lovin' Saint Augustine.'

Occasionally, she gazed out her apartment window at the clear, sunny sky, preceded on and off by a torrential downpour, before turning back to her computer.

Christmas was less than a week away. Perhaps she should purchase an artificial

Christmas tree and hang a burlap stocking on a storage shelf hook in the kitchen.

However, she told herself, she was preoccupied with bookings, so Christmas would need to be put on hold for another year. She entertained the idea of spending Christmas Day walking alone on a beach, possibly dining at one of the resort hotels afterward, before deciding on a take-out from a local cafe.

Gabe had phoned soon after Noelle returned to her apartment after the concert. At first, his messages were short, upbeat, and congratulatory, becoming longer as the days progressed, sometimes incensed, sometimes pleading with her to return his calls, always followed by an apology for missing her performance.

He'd explained he'd been detained in Wilmington, skimming over the details. And he'd never mentioned his trip to New York City, only that he'd returned to Snowing Rock and was waiting for Noelle while attending to last minute wedding preparations for his cousin, Holly. The preparations included obtaining Holly's marriage license and the resultant wait period before her vows were said.

Each time Noelle replayed his messages and heard his deep, male voice, a part of her died inside. When she'd first arrived in Snowing Rock, she'd been uninterested in a relationship with a man. She'd feared placing her trust in anyone again.

And then she had. She'd taken Gabe at his word. She'd relied on him. She'd started to let down her guard, and he'd left her for his stuntman job.

Perhaps Colin had been right all along and she truly didn't deserve happiness.

Colin's check for twenty thousand dollars arrived the morning after the concert, which she'd deposited in her bank account. The money gave her safety and security. Now, she didn't need to rely on anyone for her finances.

And, the same day her check arrived, Noelle snagged a booking agent.

However, that was the end of her good luck.

The following evening, on her walk to an artsy Cuban restaurant, she paused to stare at a billboard advertising the new blockbuster film, 'Force of Thunder Two', featuring a tough-looking, handsome man, seemingly flying through the air in a racecar. Noelle knew, without glancing at the billboard twice, that the

187

man was Gabe. Blindly, she raced back to her apartment, valiantly holding back tears until the door was safely closed behind her.

One day later, while sitting in her desk chair perusing forwarded mail, a Snowing Rock address leapt out at her. She read and reread Holly's wedding invitation, recognizing Gabe's return address on the foil-stamped response card. Remembrances of his magnificent home on Thanksgiving night flashed, and a painful tightness constricted Noelle's throat.

She'd leaned against him, with his hands wrapped around her waist, and he'd whispered, 'Noelle Wentworth, I love you. I've always loved you.'

Love. Dependability. Trust. She closed her eyes as tears streaked down her face.

Sternly, she told herself to open her eyes, marvel at the details of the embossed wedding invitation objectively, and stop crying.

She picked up a pen. On the smaller response card, she checked 'will not attend' and wrote in her name. She placed the response card in the stamped envelope, pre-addressed to Gabe. In the morning, she'd drop the card in the mailbox.

That was easy, Noelle decided, only to find herself in a crumpled heap a few minutes later, dabbing at her eyes, in that very same desk chair.

The following afternoon, Caroline called.

"Hey, Miss Saint Augustine, don't panic, but your Aunt Joy's in the hospital. We had another snowstorm and the power's been out. Anyway, your aunt took a spill inside her cottage and bruised her arm. She'll be convalescing for a few days in Snowing Rock Hospital and is in room 22, on the second floor. She can't work, and it's a few days before Christmas. I need help because I'm swamped here at the candle shop!"

"I'll phone the hospital now," Noelle hedged.

"Don't you have a round-trip plane ticket that Mr. Waters had purchased? Take the next flight from Saint Augustine to Fisher's Crossing."

Noelle stared apprehensively at her cell phone. "I don't know."

"Yup, that's a great answer," Caroline burst out, clearly annoyed. "And when you get here, you can give me an explanation as to why you're not returning his calls. He's visited the shop every day."

"Please. I don't want to discuss him again. He promised to attend my concert. I reserved a front row seat for him, I relied on him—"

"Why can't you be more understanding?" Caroline interrupted.

"I spoke with Gabe's agent."

Noelle could almost visualize Caroline throwing her head in her hands and muttering.

"Well, that explains everything," Caroline said. "Now get on the plane tomorrow and text me when you land. Alan will pick you up at Fisher's Crossing airport. Your concert's over and there are no excuses."

THE NEXT DAY, Noelle arrived in Snowing Rock. After she'd set her luggage in Aunt Joy's cottage, Noelle walked two blocks to Snowing Rock Hospital. The weather was unusually sunny, although a cold snap was predicted.

She stood outside the hospital, staring at the brightly-lit ambulance entrance sign. A woman in patterned blue scrubs walked by briskly.

"Coming inside?" the woman asked, holding the hospital's sliding glass door open.

Noelle hesitated, inhaling hospital smells of antiseptic and bleach along with her get-well arrangement of red and white spray roses that she'd purchased at the airport's gift shop.

The woman in scrubs waited expectantly and glanced at her watch.

Noelle reframed her hesitation. Yes, she was apprehensive, because entering the hospital would dredge up sad memories of her parents' deaths. On the other hand, how was she supposed to visit Aunt Joy if she didn't step inside?

Her thoughts went back to the first time she'd visited her aunt at the rehab center.

'Confront your supposed failure, view it as a learning experience, and keep moving forward,' Aunt Joy had said.

Her aunt was right. A hospital setting was an obstacle she could conquer, just as she'd rebounded from an embarrassing public concert by overcoming her fears and succeeding.

Thanking the woman in scrubs for holding the door open, Noelle walked through the entrance. She rode the elevator up to the second floor with two nurses writing notes in clipboards and conversing in low voices. Noelle quickly found room 22, and, with a deep breath, she entered her aunt's hospital room.

Aunt Joy lay sleeping in the hospital bed, looking frail and peaceful. Her favorite blue slippers were tucked beneath the bed, and a tiny Christmas tree sat on her bedside table. A TV played softly, tuned to a romantic, black and white Christmas movie starring Cary Grant.

Noelle set her bouquet on the window sill beside Gabe's exquisite copper tin get-well arrangement, filled with berry and evergreen aromatherapy scented oils, topped with a candy-cane foil bow. He'd signed the card, 'Warm Wishes For A Speedy Recovery. Best, Gabe.'

With a sigh, Noelle sat on a chair sandwiched between the bed and the window.

Aunt Joy opened her eyes and her thin face broke into a delighted smile. "My beautiful niece! Thank you for coming!"

Noelle drew her chair closer to the bed. "I came as soon as I could after Caroline called me."

"I meant, thanks for coming to the hospital," her aunt said.

"Slowly but surely, I'm learning to confront my fears." Noelle's fingers brushed against the cold stainless steel bed rail as she reached out and squeezed her aunt's hand. "More importantly, how are you?"

"Fortunately, I caught my fall, although I bruised my arm." Aunt Joy drew back the sheets and rolled up the sleeve of her hospital gown, exposing a significant bruise.

Noelle bit her bottom lip. "Oh, Aunt Joy, I'm so sorry."

"The doctor wanted to take precautions because of my age and stick me in this hospital, but I'm fine." Her aunt leaned back on the bed pillows and dismissed Noelle's concern with a sniff. "Your concert was wonderful, dear! I listened to the entire program on the radio."

"I proved to Colin I could step onto that stage and perform again."

"You didn't need to prove anything to anyone except yourself." Aunt Joy settled herself upright on the bed, then promptly asked, "Have you heard from Mr. Waters?"

Noelle stared down at her empty hands. "Yes."

"Then you know he's back in Snowing Rock." Her aunt's expression changed, and she studied Noelle in an extremely odd way. "How is he?"

"I assume he's well." Noelle pressed her lips together, determined not to ask for details, wanting to forget all about him.

"You should talk with him."

"There's nothing to say," Noelle said vaguely.

"I won't pry, although I believe he's a good man." Aunt Joy sighed, then said, "I'm getting out of the hospital in the morning."

"I'll work at the candle shop, and you can rest at the cottage all day."

"Rest?" her aunt countered. "I'm attending Holly Waters's wedding, and Caroline is picking me up early to fix my hair. Did you know Anjali's the flower girl? The flower basket is lined with organza and pearls, and Mr. Waters special-ordered it from Hollywood. Everyone in Snowing Rock is attending the wedding."

Her aunt's words hung in the silence.

Everyone in Snowing Rock was attending the wedding except her, Noelle thought with an unexplainable surge of sadness.

CHAPTER 17

E arly the next afternoon, Noelle added finishing touches to the candle shop's display window, featuring elegant white pillar candles in large hurricane vases, surrounded by loose, shiny red ornaments.

Caroline had left before lunch to pick up Aunt Joy and suggested Noelle close by one o'clock. Although Noelle had objected at first, she'd finally agreed. She planned to return to her aunt's cottage and tackle the sugar cookie recipe, this time waiting for the oven to pre-heat.

After a quick take-out lunch from Hal's Subs, Noelle tallied up the morning's receipts at the cash register. Although she'd placed a sign on the door stating that the shop was closed, she looked up as a customer walked in. Noelle regarded the lovely young woman and adorable little boy at her side. The woman's wavy chestnut hair was styled in a long pony-tail tied with a bright yellow hair bow. The style accentuated the woman's double pierced ears.

"Welcome to 'Scents of Joy'," Noelle said. "Sorry, we're closing early."

With a studious smile on her lips, the woman adjusted the large tote slung on her shoulder. "I'm here to pick up a half dozen candles on back order. Candleglow and Mistletoe."

Noelle's head jerked up. Her stomach clenched. She openly stared at the young woman with the hazel eyes highlighted with gold specks. "And ... and your name?" Noelle asked, although she already knew. Heavens above, she already knew.

"Holly Waters. And this is my son, Devin. We arrived a few days ago, along with my fiancé, John, and John's older sister, Sarah. Gabe and Sarah are the witnesses for my wedding."

Noelle nodded, then smiled at the little boy before turning to Holly. "The candles arrived last evening, although I assumed you'd received them already. I'll check."

196

As Noelle walked to the back storage room, she silently cursed the ever-efficient Caroline who'd promised to call Gabe and arrange pick-up when Noelle wasn't at the shop.

Noelle found the candles, took them to the counter, and placed them in a shopping bag. Holly accepted the bag with a 'thank you' and settled Devin on the floor near the register. She dropped to her knees and handed him a coloring book and crayons from her tote bag. When she stood, she studied Noelle for a moment.

"What do you know about my cousin, Gabe?" she asked.

Well, Noelle thought, he was charming and certainly hard-working, and up until the concert, dependable, although Noelle didn't share her thoughts aloud. She merely met Holly's persistent stare with silence.

Holly plunked her hands on her slim hips. "How strange. I've heard you're a woman who's hell-bent on succeeding, yet you accept defeat without putting up the smallest struggle."

Noelle shifted, glancing at the time. "Don't you have a wedding to prepare for?"

Holly shrugged. "Gabe's arranging all the details. He's a planner." She shook her head. "He won't be happy I came here."

197

Noelle stared blankly at the display window. "If this is about him not attending my concert, I don't want to talk about it."

Holly sighed and took Noelle's hands in hers. "What happened in Wilmington is tearing Gabe apart. And from the haunted look on your face, you're not doing any better."

"He's so dedicated to his job, I know it will always come first." Noelle pulled from Holly's grip. "Besides, it doesn't matter."

"Listen, it does matter." Holly's tone rose. "And both of you aren't going to ruin my wedding by being miserable!"

"I'm not attending your wedding and—"

"Noelle." Holly's face grew speculative. "I thought you and Gabe were growing close, but you really don't know ... do you?"

"Know what?"

Holly put her hands on Noelle's arms. "After Gabe finished the film shoot, he was rushed to Wilmington Hospital because of a diabetes complication. His blood sugar dropped too low because he didn't plan his meals correctly. The filming ran late and he was in a hurry to see you so he didn't bother to eat." Holly released her grip. "Obviously, he missed his flight to Saint Augustine."

Noelle touched a hand to her mouth. Her mind registered shock. "Diabetes? Gabe? He never mentioned —"

Holly gave a bemused smile. "He wants everyone to think he's this strapping, tough guy. Truth is, he was very sick when he was young. His parents were negligent and he wasn't diagnosed with Type I diabetes until he was eleven years old. Since then, he's always been trying to prove himself."

"Why didn't he tell me?"

"Maybe he was waiting to explain in person. I've lived with him the last few days and he wants to see you, although he's not about to approach you again. He's too proud and stubborn."

Noelle's voice caught. She swallowed. "There's so much I want to say to him."

"That's why you're coming with me so you can attend my wedding."

"I ... I sent in my response card stating I couldn't —"

"And I'm the bride and overruling your response card. My car is parked outside the candle shop."

"I can't go to a wedding looking like this." Noelle rubbed her hands across her gray wool sweater and navy slacks. "I need to change. I'd bought a new dress, but it's at my aunt's cottage."

Holly bent to pick up Devin's crayons and coloring book and grabbed his hand. "Then what're we waiting for? I can't be late for my own wedding!"

NOELLE REGARDED her reflection in the cottage's bedroom mirror, buttoning a faux-fur jacket over her red sequined dress. She'd grinned at the henna tattoo peeking through the sheer sleeve of her dress. Although the tattoo had faded, the words were still prominent.

'Running away from your problems is a race you'll never win.'

With that thought, the knot in her stomach began to dissolve, and a few minutes later she pronounced herself ready. Black tights kept her legs warm, and she'd added red pom-poms to her black leather ankle boots for a wintry, festive air. She'd pulled her hair back from her forehead, the way Gabe liked, secured at the crown with a sparkly hair clip. Soft blonde curls framed her heart-shaped face, and pearl stud earrings completed her outfit.

She'd changed quickly while Holly and Devin waited inside Aunt Joy's cottage.

Now, an hour later, Noelle walked to the entrance of Gabe's barn where the wedding was being held. Holly had dropped Noelle off before driving on to Gabe's house to get ready. Holly had kept the bag of Candleglow and Mistletoe candles, saying she wanted them for her new home.

Darkness had fallen, and Noelle regarded the large, rustic barn doors lit by a twinkling string of bistro lights. She hesitated, trying to calm herself. What would Gabe say when he saw her? Would he demand she leave? Or worse, would he simply ignore her, his handsome face disinterested, yet cordial?

And what if Lucia were his date?

With resolve, Noelle pulled her mind away from defeating thoughts. He'd once told her he loved her, that he was a patient man, and would wait for her.

Her muscles tightened in readiness. She'd come this far and, if he gave her a moment, she'd apologize for misjudging him. All she would ask was a few minutes of his time.

201

Noelle stepped inside the barn and gasped at the gorgeous interior decorated in a wintry design theme. Blue ambient lighting transformed the large space into an icy hue, calling to mind a romantic winter fairyland. Crystal strands of garland dripped from a glittering chandelier hanging in the center. Silver tablecloths were draped over six long tables, shimmering beneath the warm glow of Candleglow and Mistletoe candles. Fresh rosemary, wrapped in burlap, was used as place cards for each table setting, and clear glass chargers framed gleaming white china.

Noelle wandered to the cake table on a rollable stand displaying a five-tiered pink wedding cake. Pink and white fondant roses cascaded down the front of the cake, and pink rose petals were sprinkled on the scalloped frosting. Mrs. Fernandez was certainly a gifted cake decorator, and white sheer curtains and a silver candelabrum added an elegant backdrop.

In addition, ten vanilla scented beeswax votive candles encircled the cake. Noelle grinned. Gabe had planned the occasion perfectly.

She glanced at her watch, knowing she was early. A violinist and keyboard player setting up their instruments, along with uniformed caterers from Snowing Rock Country Club, nodded to her. The clergyman stood at the front by the altar. He looked out an arched picture window to acres of wintry pastureland lit by moonlight.

Sprigs of fir branches hung from the backs of chairs that were set, ceremony style, facing the altar. White orchids in tall silver stands flanked the aisle.

Noelle hung her coat on a coat rack near the entrance and took an aisle seat in the back row. Soon afterward, the wedding guests filed in. Caroline, Alan, and Aunt Joy installed themselves in the vacant seats in Noelle's row, along with Mr. and Mrs. Fernandez.

Aunt Joy's gray hair was coiled in a low bun. True to her non-conformist style, she'd added a crown of shiny green leaves, which didn't match her bohemian style purple gown.

Aunt Joy's face was wreathed in a wide smile. "I'm thrilled you decided to attend, dear. You made a wise decision."

"I had a change of heart, along with some encouragement from the bride," Noelle replied.

With two opening blasts of organ chords from the keyboard player, the clergyman and John, the groom, took their places at the altar.

Sarah, the only bridesmaid, walked down the aisle alone, followed by Anjali and Devin. Anjali's dark face gleamed with joy, her red plaid dress and black patent leather shoes fitting to perfection. She proudly held up her organza flower basket, skipping down the aisle while tugging on Devin's hand.

When the wedding march began playing, all the guests stood to watch Holly walk slowly down the aisle escorted by Gabe. She wore a short, embroidered, white lace gown with bell sleeves, her hair in the same pony-tail style she'd worn earlier at the candle shop. Gabe looked unbearably handsome, resplendent in an elegant black tuxedo hugging his tall, powerful frame.

Noelle stood a mere foot away from him as he passed, her hands tightly bracing the seat in front of her. She wanted to rely on his undeniably strong presence. Trusting him. Loving him.

GABE STOOD SILENTLY at the altar during the service. Holly and John's marriage vows held a keen sense of regret for him, because he'd debated asking Noelle to marry him only a few weeks earlier on Thanksgiving night.

A hollowness filled his chest. So much had changed in just a few short weeks.

Scarcely turning his head, he viewed the crowded rows, moving past Caroline and Alan. He greeted Mr. and Mrs. Fernandez with an appreciative nod, and grinned as his gaze went by Aunt Joy wearing an outrageous shiny green crown on her head, then to a beautiful blonde woman in a red sequined dress sitting at the end of the row.

His heart leapt, pounding wildly as a pair of gorgeous jade-green eyes locked with his.

He tore his gaze away. Noelle was in Snowing Rock! Despite her response card stating 'no', she'd come to the wedding after all.

Briefly, he closed his eyes. Why was she here?

She hadn't answered his numerous calls. She hadn't been interested. What had she meant when she'd told both Mrs. Fernandez and Caroline that she loved Saint Augustine?

His pride demanded he meet her stare with bland indifference, showing he was through pleading with her.

His heart, however, didn't agree with his pride.

'I'm slowly learning to trust again,' she'd said quietly. 'Give me time.'

He opened his eyes and found her gaze. Her lips parted and she smiled, her expression beseeching. Silently, she was asking him for a second chance.

He hardly stirred, could scarcely take a breath. Long ago, he'd been mesmerized by a brave young woman who'd been immersed in a posh musical world that a guy like him, from the other side of town, had never known existed. And now, fifteen years later, he longed to hear Noelle say what he read in her expressive green eyes.

'I love you.'

And he loved her, with an affection that had only increased over the years.

Briefly, he contemplated striding down the aisle and escorting her to the altar, requesting that the clergyman marry them alongside his cousin and new husband.

No, Gabe quickly decided. That wasn't fair to Noelle. His courageous, talented woman deserved her own exquisite wedding.

The fanfare recessional music struck a majestic cadence and, with a start, Gabe realized the ceremony was over. He waited for the bride and groom, followed by Anjali and Devin, before he walked down the aisle beside Sarah.

Looking through the celebratory, milling crowd, he spotted Noelle nodding and smiling with Caroline. A caterer, behind a cart, poured glasses of pink champagne, while Caroline scooped up several coconut breaded shrimp.

When Gabe reached them, he flashed a polite, dismissive greeting to Caroline.

She grabbed her champagne glass. "Good to see you, too, Mr. Waters," Caroline laughed and walked away.

He dragged air into his lungs and turned to face Noelle, pausing to feast his gaze on her. She looked like the exquisite goddess in a red sequined dress that he'd dreamed about, and she was heartbreakingly stunning.

He cleared his throat. "Champagne?" he asked.

"I'll wait."

"May we speak for a moment?"

"Yes, of course," she said.

He kept her close to his side, leading her to the barn door entrance. He lowered his head and whispered against her soft, blonde hair. "I've missed you very, very much."

Her taffeta skirt rustled gracefully as she turned to face him. "I've missed you, too."

"I'm sorry I wasn't there for your performance."

"I know," she said softly.

"You played brilliantly. I listened to the entire concert on the radio the day afterward on a delayed broadcast. Does that count?"

She laughed, despite the tears misting her eyes. "Please, don't apologize."

He drew her nearer. Gently, he brushed a shining curl from her cheek, then glanced around. "There are too many people here," he said. "My cousin won't mind if we leave the reception early."

"She might. She's the one who brought me here."

He scowled. "Holly?"

"Yes, she stopped at the candle shop this afternoon. She told me about what happened to you in Wilmington."

The back of his throat ached. Mentally, he debated about thanking Holly or being outraged that she'd interfered in his personal affairs.

"What did she say?" He tried to keep his tone casual.

"Everything." Noelle breathed after a long pause. "And I'm so relieved you're well."

He nodded a curt acceptance and took her hand.

"Where are we going?" Noelle asked. "I'd love a piece of Mrs. Fernandez's pink champagne wedding cake."

"We'll be back on time for champagne and wedding cake," he assured.

Noelle retrieved her coat from the coat rack near the doorway.

He slipped her coat around her shoulders and offered a slow grin. "There's something at my house I'd like to show you. An early Christmas gift."

CHAPTER 18

The ride from the barn to Gabe's house took less than five minutes. They sat outside in the Land Rover while the engine idled and the heat blasted.

He sat silent, studying her.

She looked down at her hands. "I don't know how to begin. I only know I want a fresh start."

"Let's begin with truthfulness. You told me once you were slowly learning to trust again. Do you trust me now?"

She nodded.

"Then why didn't you answer my calls after the concert?"

She gave a little sigh. "I ... couldn't. I was so disappointed you weren't in the audience. Between my parents' deaths and my bad marriage, I assumed you'd let me down, just like everyone else."

"I'd never intentionally let you down, all right?" His hazel eyes held hers as he continued. "And then there's the matter of Thanksgiving evening when we were standing on my balcony together. Do you remember what I said?"

She looked up at him. "Yes."

"Then shall we try again?" He tilted up her chin. "I've been waiting for a more fitting reply."

She nodded, her voice too choked with tears to speak.

He cradled her face in his hands. "Noelle Wentworth, I love you."

She lay her trembling hand against his cheek. "I love you, too."

He grinned. "Much better."

She attempted to grin in return, which was thwarted by tears of elation streaking down her cheeks.

He wiped her tears with his fingers and his lips captured hers.

Intent on showing him how much she loved him, Noelle returned his kisses with all the happiness in her heart. By the time the kiss ended, the SUV's windows were fogged. He kept his arms around her while they both waited for their breathing to slow.

He kissed her forehead. "Shall we go into the house?"

Unwilling to end their discussion yet, she bit her lip and hesitated. "I have a question, too."

His dark brows drew together. "Go ahead."

"Why didn't you tell me about your diabetes? If I'd known—"

"I felt ashamed," he said. "You saw me fifteen years ago as a skinny, defenseless kid who needed protecting. I didn't want to appear even weaker in your eyes."

"Diabetes doesn't make you weak. You're brave, overcoming great obstacles and succeeding. Holly said you've managed your diabetes since you were a child."

He nodded soberly. "Yes, and if I take care of myself, there's no problem. However, because of my hectic schedule, I've made a decision." He transferred his gaze to his home, then Noelle. "I'm slowing down my stunt work and devoting more time to my teen outreach center."

He hadn't mentioned devoting more time to her, Noelle reflected. And there was something else she wanted to ask him. He'd flown to New York City and must've seen Lucia.

Noelle waved an airy hand in her mind, refusing to abandon all her dignity.

They'd reconciled. Everything was settled. They both wanted a fresh start.

A few moments later, they stepped inside the large foyer of his home. Gabe took her coat, as well as his own, hanging both in the entry closet.

Noelle looked up and smiled. A mistletoe was strategically placed in the doorway leading to the living room.

"Did you plan this?" She exaggerated an accusing look at him.

He chuckled. "I hung the mistletoe when I returned from Wilmington, because I was hopeful you'd be joining me here. However, when I received your response card that you wouldn't be attending Holly's wedding, I planned to take the mistletoe down. Then, between the eleventh-hour wedding preparations and the company, I forgot." He offered a guilty shrug. "Sometimes it's better not to be a planner."

She laughed.

He glanced up at the mistletoe. "Shall we?" He gathered her in his arms for a passionate kiss, leaving her trembling and straining to be nearer him.

He lifted his lips and threaded his fingers through her hair. "Did you miss me?"

"More than you can imagine."

His thumbs caressed her cheekbones. "Are you ready to see your gift?" He escorted her into the living room and flicked on the low, overhead light. "Sorry, it was too large to wrap."

Noelle stood stock-still. She blinked, staring at the black, glossy, baby grand piano and matching bench arranged at an angle, between the floor to ceiling windows and the fireplace.

"This piano looks just like mine," she murmured.

"That's because it is," he responded with a hint of amusement in his voice. He walked to the fireplace mantel and lit a half dozen candles.

Noelle shook her head. "My piano is in storage in New York City ..." Even as she spoke, she began walking toward the piano, slowly at first, then faster.

With Gabe striding behind her, she sat at the bench and checked the fallboard. Beneath were her engraved initials, N.W.

She whirled. "When? How?"

"After I missed your concert and was discharged from Wilmington Hospital, I flew directly to New York City. I'd arranged to get your piano out of storage and ship it to Snowing Rock and wanted to double-check that it was yours. A couple of weeks ago, I'd asked your Aunt Joy, and she assisted me in locating the storage facility."

"Aunt Joy never mentioned anything, although she encouraged me to talk to you."

"We both agree your aunt is a remarkable woman." He lowered his head and his mouth parted Noelle's for a deep, long kiss. When he lifted his lips, he whispered, "I want my own private piano concert, all right?"

The husky tone of his request sent a jolt up Noelle's spine.

He sat on the bench beside her with one arm around her shoulders. "With all the free time I'll have, will you teach me how to play the piano?"

"I thought you were tone-deaf."

"I know where middle C is." He struck the white key with his free hand.

She glanced up at his smiling, indignant expression. "I've thought about teaching piano when I'm not helping my aunt in the candle shop," she said.

He traced her engraved initials on the shiny fallboard with his fingertips. "It's a good thing your last initial is the same as mine. Otherwise, I'd have to buy you a new piano."

His tone was light, although Noelle heard the roughness in his voice.

"What do you mean?"

"Besides piano lessons and volunteering at my outreach center, I'll want to devote my time to my beautiful wife." He looked meaningfully at her. "Noelle Wentworth, will you marry me? I can't begin to comprehend my life without you."

"Yes." She snuggled closer and locked her hands around his powerful shoulders. "Gabe Waters, my answer is yes."

"We can be married on Christmas Day," he said.

"You can't be serious." Noelle sighed. "We'll need time to plan and prepare."

"All right, I'm a patient man," he nodded with a grin. "We'll wait until New Year's Day. We'll book everyone tonight when we return to my cousin's reception. The cake decorator, the clergyman, the musicians, and the caterers are all there. Will the barn be all right for the ceremony and reception? You know I'm usually a planner."

216

Tears of happiness welled in her eyes. "Yes, perfect."

He stood, extended his hand, and nodded toward the piano bench. "I wonder if there's any Christmas music in there."

Surprised by his suddenly somber tone, she eyed him quizzically before she stood and lifted the lid of the bench. "I'd stored old sheet music, but doubt there's any Christmas music."

"Keep digging," he prodded.

A small, blue Tiffany box stopped her short.

She glanced at him and he nodded for her to continue. She lifted out the box. When she unsnapped the lid, a magnificent diamond ring glittered in the glow of the candles.

In a soft voice, he said, "I hope you like the ring. It's not as beautiful as you, but—"

She stared at the ring in awe, admiring the shiny, flawless sparkle. Poignant tears filled her eyes.

"Merry Christmas, Noelle." He slipped the ring onto her finger.

She wanted to tell him that he was generous and thoughtful, that his exquisite ring was gorgeous, and that she trusted him completely. All she could manage to say through her tears was, "Merry Christmas, Gabe."

He crushed her to his chest. Assaulted by his intense kisses, her senses whirled.

Because for this man she adored, her love was as sweet and warm as a holiday candle.

THE END

A NOTE FROM THE AUTHOR

Thank you for reading *Candleglow and Mistletoe!* I hope you enjoyed it. If you did, please help other people find this book and write a review.

Visit my website at: http://josieriviera.com
and sign up for my newsletter.
As a thank-you, I'll send you a free sweet romance novella.

And, watch and share the book trailer here: https://youtu.be/CIqmFKRXIqY

ABOUT THE AUTHOR

Josie Riviera is a *USA TODAY* Bestselling Author of contemporary, inspirational, and historical sweet romances that read like Hallmark movies. She lives in the Charlotte, NC, area with her wonderfully supportive husband. They share their home with an adorable Shih Tzu who constantly needs grooming and live in an old house forever needing renovations.

OTHER BOOKS BY JOSIE RIVIERA

A Snowy White Christmas

I Love You More

Seeking Patience

Seeking Catherine

We'd Rather Be Writing

Made in the USA
Middletown, DE
17 October 2017